A SENSE OF THE SEA

SEA

and other stories

#debuke2

Annmarie Miles

© Annmarie Miles 2018

Introduction

I was flattered and delighted to be asked to introduce this work. I was lucky enough to hear Annmarie Miles read her prize-winning story Blessed Assurance at the Junefest Literary Festival in 2014. Total silence reigned for a moment as she drew to a close. I am delighted to read it again in this new collection of flash and micro-fiction; it is as moving on the page as it was in the flesh.

For Annmarie's greatest gift is her optimism, her deep and gentle Christian faith, and her belief in the inherent goodness of mankind, despite so much current evidence to the contrary. There is a little more darkness in this, her second collection, and a few of the stories have a little sting in the tail, but overall the sensation is of joy and humour against adversity.

To dip in and out of this collection, in quiet moments, is a gentle and uplifting reading experience. Leave behind the coarseness and violence of the headlines and remind yourself that under the skin, we remain as we have always been, hopeful and joyful, hard-working and full of love. And allow yourself tiny shouts of celebration as we draw close to the final words of the story of young Billy Tongs, and of the closing piece, Malcolm Fulcrum; I guarantee a smile on your face!

Orla McAlinden
Award winning writer of
'The Flight of the Wren' and 'The Accidental Wife'
November 2018

Author Bio

Born and raised in Tallaght, in the foothills of South County Dublin, now living in the Eastern Valley of Gwent in South Wales, Annmarie Miles was *'raised on songs and stories'*.

She has been blogging nonfiction at auntyamo.com since 2012. She writes long and short fiction, as well as having experience in web content creation and radio presenting. She is a regular contributor to VOX Magazine in Ireland, and the Association of Christian Writers blog in the UK.

In 2016 her first collection of short stories 'The Long & The Short of it' was shortlisted for the inaugural Carousel Aware Prize for Independent Authors. Her short stories have also made other award lists, including the RTÉ/Penguin Short Story competition and the Jonathan Swift Creative Writing Award.

Annmarie is married to Richard, who is a church minister. They live surrounded by books, gadgets and fridge magnets!

You can find Annmarie on social media by looking for *amowriting*. She blogs about her faith at www.auntyamo.com and you can find more about her books on www.annmariemiles.co.uk

Dedication

For Betty & Christy
(Ma & Da)

A Sense of the Sea and other stories

2018

© Annmarie Miles

Cover design by Tallaght Echo Design

Acknowledgements

To readers of stories and blogposts, I'm only here because you're here.

To my many writing friends across the world, be they online or face to face – keep scribbling.

My thanks to Orla McAlinden for her encouraging words. Orla is a rising talent with her feet firmly on the ground – she inspires me.

I must make special mention of Karenne Griffin, who listens to me ramble on about my ideas, then helps me whip them into shape.

To Tallaght Echo Design for the book cover.

To my 7 siblings, 27 *niblings*, and their associated millions – I love you.

To my husband Richard, who continues to encourage me to take the time to write, especially when I'm fed up and forget how much I love it.

To God, who inspires me by The Greatest Story Ever Told, and has made me a part of it.
Unless the Lord builds the house ... Psalm 127v1.

Contents

A Sense of the Sea
(First Published National Flash Fiction Day (NFFD) Flashflood 2014)

Nazar loved the sea. He loved the feel of cold water on his feet and squishy sand between his toes. He loved the rush of water around his ankles and the pull of the outgoing wave. His other love was stones. He was an expert at spotting the unusual. Nazar recognised every shade and line; every curve and rough corner.

He rarely saw others on the beach; a woman walking her dog, a man with his child. Never before had he seen the camper van.

He went to investigate. As he got close to the van, a man opened the door. Nazar wanted to walk away, but the man called out to him before he could turn around. In a moment of uncertainty, Nazar froze. He blinked a couple of times, and the man was standing in front of him. He was talking quickly and Nazar couldn't catch all he was saying.

"Slow down," said Nazar. "You need to slow down; I don't know what you're saying."

"You can't understand English?" Camper Van Man replied, in exaggerated syllables.

"I can understand it. I just can't hear it! If you take your time I can read your lips."

"Ahhh, okay. Well, I just thought I'd take a walk along the water's edge. Want to come with me?"

Nazar was interested in the man and even though it broke his mum's rule about strangers, he agreed.

"Why is your camper van on the beach?"

"My girl and I, we're travelling poets. You like poetry?"

Nazar shrugged a reply. "Not really."

"What do you like?"

"Stones."

"Sorry mate, I thought you said stones. Come again?"

"I did say stones." Nazar waved his bucket.

"Oh, okay. Cool. Everyone has their thing."

They got to the shoreline. Nazar was already barefoot and the man didn't bother removing his sandals.

"Beautiful huh?"

"Yes," said Nazar. "It really is. I bet it sounds even better than it looks."

"Awh man, the sound is amazing. Soothing, but hurrying too. Like when you're on a rollercoaster, you know? The swell then the drop. The rush, the pause, then the rush again. It's the nearest I can tell you."

It was the best description Nazar had been given.

"So, are you a good poet?"

"I think so. I'm a happy poet. I love to write and read my poetry. Me and my girl, we go to all the festivals."

They stood in silence; letting the water race past their feet.

"I gotta go, I can hear my girl calling me. You want to meet another travelling poet?"

"No, thanks. I'd better go." Nazar held out his hand to shake hands. The man did too; above Nazar's and to the right of it. Nazar had been so busy looking at Camper Van Man's lips, he had not noticed his eyes.

Nazar moved his hand to meet the man's. "Do you want me to tell you what the sea looks like?"

"Thanks kid but I got it. Rollercoaster, right? Swell then drop, rush then calm?"

Nazar smiled. "Yeah that's it."

The Remains of the Day Job

He saw the queue from across the carpark but headed for the door anyway, just to check he was right about the opening times. Two teens in scruffy tracksuits squared up to him and he got the message. Without making eye contact, he made his way to the back of the line. With each step he felt more and more out of sync with everyone he passed. He was overdressed in his suit and good overcoat.

When he got up that morning it had never occurred to him not to wear the suit. He always wore a suit, unless it was the weekend. Clean shirt and a well-chosen tie; it was Monday, what else would he wear? He'd been dressing like this every weekday morning for forty years.

Here, he was the only one in a suit. There were some dressed in what his former head of HR would have called 'smart casual', but most were wearing jeans or track suits.

There was a shuffle up ahead and by the time he started walking towards the door, there was a queue of people as long behind him. The nearer he got to the entrance, the less order the queue held. He found himself in a group of people surging towards the door, everyone trying to elbow ahead of the person next to them. He found himself at the back, having put up no resistance, and was now behind most people who had joined the queue after him.

Slowly he made his way to the reception desk, and it was his turn.

"Good morning, my name is Charles Fitzmaurice. On March the 26th ..."

"Is this your first time here?" The receptionist's eyes never left her computer screen.

"I'm sorry? Oh, not exactly, you see my name is ..."

"Have you ever signed on here before?"

3

Now she was looking at him in a way that made him wish she wasn't.

"Well no, I haven't. You see my name is ..."

"Section A, take a number and wait to be called. NEXT?"

Charles wondered should he try again, but the complaints of the tracksuit next in line compelled him to move away from the desk.

Not sure which way to turn, he scanned the area. It was large with two open sections. The reception desk he'd briefly visited was in the middle. High ceilings, with windows at the very top that let in lots of light. The light didn't make it all the way to the floor, and the darkness suited the mood of most of those waiting. Whitewashed walls had chrome chairs bolted to them. Then there were rows of the same chairs facing a line of metal kiosks.

Both sides were almost identical, and he looked for some evidence of Section A. Most of the people who'd been in the queue with him had formed another line towards one of the kiosks. The other dozen were empty. He was relieved to see that that was Section C, and found Section A on the other side.

There were still plenty of people, but all were seated in the rows, bar one or two sitting at computer desks in the far corner. Charles searched for a ticket machine. He found it and tucking his folder under his arm, tried to wrestle a ticket off the roll. He ended up with four. He pulled the bottom one off, tearing it in half. His folder started to slip, so he moved it between his knees and proceeded to rescue the other half of his ticket. He then tried to tuck the superfluous tickets back into the machine. By the time he took a seat, he was sweating. For the first time in his life, his collar and tie seemed uncomfortable.

He took his coat off and threw it over his arm. Cooling down a little, he watched the numbers slowly change and get closer to the number he held, in two pieces. His number was 76, so at 74 he checked his folder and his tie were straight and stood ready. After twenty minutes he sat down again. 75 popped up and he braced himself for another wait, when 76 popped up straight away.

4

He made his way to the kiosk and took a seat. The woman behind the counter was still typing away.

"Good morning," he said. "My name is…" Before Charles got any further, the woman was up off her chair. "Bear with me …" and she was gone.

Charles looked around at the metal that surrounded him, then through the Perspex window to the busy office on the other side. He wished he was sitting at his old desk. To be on the phone to people, taking enquiries, arranging meetings, updating spreadsheets.

When the woman returned she had an armful of forms. "Right," she said, dumping the forms on the desk. "Sorry about that. You're a first timer yeah? I'll need you to fill out one of these, and one of these." She wrestled the forms out of the pile on the desk and started to fill an empty plastic file holder with the rest.

"Actually, I don't need those. You see my name is …"

"Have you recently left a job or been made redundant?"

"Well, yes but …"

"And have you made a claim for unemployment benefit yet?"

"Well, no but …"

"Then you'll have to fill in these forms, so I can process your claim."

"But I don't want to claim, I have another job already – in fact I should be there now."

"So why are you here then?" Exasperated, she continued to shove the spare forms into the divider.

"Well, my name is Charles Fitzmaurice. I finished my job on March 26th."

"Yes, AND?"

"I left my bicycle helmet behind and I need it."

"What are you doing here then?"

"Well this is where I used to work. In fact, I can see it hanging on the coat stand. If you could just pass it to me, that would be great. I really need to get to my new job."

5

Requiescat in Pace

Arthur had heard the thump but thought nothing of it. After 15 minutes when she still wasn't back, and the potatoes were boiling over, he called her to let her know they needed turning down. He got to the bottom of the stairs, opened his mouth to say her name, but the air was sucked out of his lungs at the sight of her. Face down halfway up the stairs, the pile of freshly ironed pillow cases strewn everywhere.

He took the first step and said her name, though no sound came out. Then he was beside her, trying to fit between her and the bannister. Her eyes and mouth were wide open, she looked as surprised as he was to be gone.

The water was boiling with fury now, the lid banging off the pot, fuelled by heat and steam; demanding attention. He thought he should turn it off, that's what she would do. He went back down the stairs and into the kitchen and turned the switch. Immediately the lid was still and quiet. He watched the bubbles flatten then went back to the stairs.

He didn't move again until it was too dark to see her. He had been holding her hand all that time and it was difficult to let it go now. He liked that. He was sore and stiff from sitting at an awkward angle beside her. He limped to the light switch and turned it on.

"What will I do Fran? What now? Help me. You always know best. You're my Fran with the plan." He began to cry. "Tell me love, tell me what to do."

He waited a long time, but no answer came.

He wandered back into the kitchen and strained the cold potatoes. He threw a lump of butter in the pot and ate half of them, leaving the rest for Fran. Then he made two mugs of tea and went back to the stairs.

As he drank, his mind went back to their wedding. A day of joyful simplicity. That night their excitement turned to nervous fumbling. They'd never seen each other before. After an hour, they gave up and decided to make some tea; sitting in their dressing gowns, they talked long into the night. "That was the best night of my life, Art," she used to say. His cheeky reply was always, "until the next night." He smiled at the memory of old pleasures.

He looked at her again, fully expecting her to smile back at him as she always did, but her face was captured in its final expression.

When he got cold he dragged the blanket from the end of the bed and put it around her as best he could, then he got under what was left of it. He wasn't comfortable enough to sleep, but he couldn't leave her.

He must have dozed at some stage as the sound of the milkman stirred him. He tried to stand but couldn't steady himself. He was disappointed Fran made no effort to help him, and didn't urge him to be careful. He put the kettle on again and ate the other half of the potatoes while he waited for it to boil. When it did he made one mug of tea and picked up the phone.

"Frances, it's Daddy. Your mammy, your ma…"

Arthur never finished the sentence. He was still holding the phone sobbing like a lost child, when his daughter let herself in. The next hours, days and weeks were a blur. And though his gravestone says he lived another seven years, those closest to him would tell you, Arthur and Fran died the same day.

Way Too Long

The grey Ford Cortina and Broad Hill were old enemies, but the car never failed to reach the small church at the top, despite one or two close calls over the years. The Reverend Wayne Toovey-Longbridge came to a sudden stop when the wheels hit the kerb.

"Perfect," he said, leaving the car in gear. He wrestled with the steering wheel lock and eventually secured the car to his liking. He propped his pork pie hat a little skew-whiff on his flat head; it never felt right, but he could not be seen without it. With his large-print Bible under his arm, he headed for the church.

He loved his annual visit to St. Polycarp's. It was one of the highlights of his preaching schedule. He had been the special guest speaker at their anniversary weekend service for over thirty-five years. Their welcome was always warm, the gift always generous, and Dolly Jenkins' Bakewell slice was always scrumptious. He was looking forward to it already.

As he climbed the hill to the main entrance of the church building, he could hear rock music from a nearby window.

"Such a din," he tutted. "And on a Sunday."

He got to the church door and realised the music was not coming from a nearby window, but from inside the church. He was so discombobulated that he missed the church notice board. This was probably a good thing as his name had been creatively edited by someone and so the notice read: 'The preacher for our anniversary service this Sunday will be Way Too Long.'

The Reverend stepped in the doorway of what used to be the vestibule. He immediately disliked it. It was brightly painted; soft furnishings replaced the wood and brass he remembered. Through to the sanctuary it was worse. Most of the pews were gone. The ones that remained were covered with bright cushions. The rest of the

9

seating consisted of chairs in rows of semicircles. No middle aisle. There were also some beanbags in a corner. Where the old wooden pulpit and steps used to be was a platform with lighting and a Perspex lectern. A large flat screen covered most of the back wall, where Mrs Ottery's cross-stitched mural of the miracles of Jesus used to be.

"Welcome to Polly's!" A teenager in ripped jeans and a floppy hat came bounding down towards the Reverend, his arm already thrust out for the handshake. The Reverend reached out too but only to lean against something, as the ground wobbled beneath him. The teen led him to a nearby armchair.

"Oh dear. Are you okay?" He waved and shouted, "Will, we've got a fainter."

The Reverend composed himself, to see another young man walk towards him. "Reverend Longbridge?"

"Eh, yes. I think so."

"I'm Will Power. I'm the new Pastor here."

The Reverend extended a hand slowly. "Will Power?"

"I know," said Will, shaking hands with vigour. "I've heard all the jokes, but there's a fiver in it for anyone who can come up with a new one."

The floppy hat and Will Power burst into a fit of laughing.

Reverend Longbridge didn't. "I didn't know they had installed a minister here."

"Oh no, didn't you get the email? What a shame. Well we had a wonderful induction day. We relaunched the church, and as you see, we've done the place up a bit."

"Indeed." The Reverend was at a loss for words. He could not stop thinking about poor Mrs Ottery and the hard work she had done on the mural. Then something occurred to him. "You probably don't need me today then."

"Oh yes, of course we do." Will wasn't pretending. "Everyone here knows that Polly's, sorry St Polycarp's, anniversary wouldn't be the same without you. And I'm all for keeping some traditions alive."

Had the Reverend the energy, he would have asked which ones.

As Will and the floppy hat led the Reverend past the platform he noticed a drum kit, two guitars and several microphones. He was somewhat consoled to see the organ there too.

"I see you've kept Mr Jones' old Hammond organ," said the Reverend.

"Oh yes," said the floppy hat. "The sound out of it is amazing. Like a cross between The Brooklyn Tabernacle Choir and The Doors."

The Reverend felt faint again and was glad to be led into a room that was familiar. The vestry had not been touched in the refurbishment and for that he was grateful.

"I'll leave you to your preparations," said Will. "There's some water and a glass on the table."

"Unless you'd like a latte?" the floppy hat piped up.

"No thank you. You can come and get me just before the start, but I'd like some quiet time until then."

"No problem Rev," said Will, and they were gone.

The Reverend sank to his knees and put his head in his hands. He suddenly felt far from God, and had no words to say to his unusually distant Maker. He stayed on his knees and said the Lord's prayer. It seemed to open a channel, but his intercessions lacked the usual fervency. Over and over he asked God to help him. He felt irrelevant; his thoughts on the story of the loaves and fishes were fuzzy. They seemed disconnected to the altered venue. He heard a tap on the door and raised his eyes to heaven with one more silent plea. He struggled to his feet and wiped the dust from his trousers.

Floppy hat led him to a seat. The lights were so bright, he was unable to see if there were one or one hundred people in the congregation. He closed his eyes and continued his intercessions when he heard Will Power calling the service to order.

He looked up as some of the lights dimmed and like a vision from heaven itself, Mrs Ottery's mural appeared in front of him. He blinked a few times to refresh his vision, but there it was, projected onto the screen. He listened to Will announce the new 'Virtual Tribal Bible study groups', and make a plea to the youth group not to set the toilet roll on fire again this week. The Reverend kept his eyes on the mural, its familiarity brought him peace.

"Let's stand to sing," said Will.

The Reverend struggled to his feet, hoping the drums wouldn't be too loud, when he heard the pealing chords of the introduction of his favourite hymn, *Great is Thy Faithfulness*. As he sang his strength increased. By the last verse of the hymn, when Will gave him the nod to come up to the front, he was refreshed and renewed; taking the two small steps to the platform with as much vigour as his knees would allow.

He read the passage from his old Bible: the story of Jesus using a small amount of bread and fish to feed a large number of people. He still could not see much beyond the front row, where Will was seated beside the floppy hat. After he finished the reading, he led the congregation in prayer and it was only when he heard the loud 'Amen' did he realise how full the church was. He stood in silence for a minute or so, which must have felt longer to Will and the floppy hat as they exchanged panicked glances. Will was just about to stand and intervene when Reverend lifted his hand to calm him.

"I'm sorry dear friends," said the Reverend, "for my hesitation in speaking. For a minute, I forgot what I wanted to say. No, that's not true, I didn't forget the words. I forgot for a moment that they are as relevant in this transformed building as they have ever been. When I saw this new place, I worried I had nothing relevant to say. Nothing that could impress or inspire. Nothing that could compete with the dazzling lights of this place. I forgot these are not my words but God's. And as Jesus took the meagre lunch of a small boy and transformed it into a meal that would nourish a multitude, so I trust he will do the same for this old man and his feeble words."

The Reverend Wayne Toovey-Longbridge went on to deliver what would go down as the best sermon he'd ever preached. No one knew if it was as long as his usual sermons, because no one noticed the time.

Afterwards the congregation stood around drinking lattes, as Dolly Jenkins passed around her Bakewell slices. The Reverend spoke to as many as he could, embracing old friends and being introduced to new ones. When there were just a few left, moving chairs for the following morning's toddler group meeting, the Reverend stood at the main church door with Will.

"Mrs Ottery would be happy she's still part of the furniture," said the Reverend, smiling.

"I'd have loved to keep the mural," said Will. "But when we took it down to paint the wall, it fell apart. We were so upset. Thankfully we'd had lots of good photos taken before the work started. So, in a way we were able to preserve it. I hope you're not cross about it."

"Not at all Will. I'm sorry if I was a bit, well, off at the beginning. I had no idea of any of these changes. They surprised me, and to be honest they frightened me."

"You? Frightened?" said Will. "I can hardly believe it. What hope is there for me if you're afraid? I'm terrified. I don't know what to do with all these people. I don't know if I have what it takes to change this community. How can I minister to this neighbourhood? I'm not sure I'm enough."

"Have you forgotten what I preached already? That's the point son, you're not enough," said the Reverend pointing at Will with his hat. "Any real and lasting transformation comes from God himself." He was now pointing at the sky.

"Absolutely, you're right," Will said as the Reverend started to make his way back to his car.

"Of course, I'm right. Real change needs more than just … will power you know," the Reverend said with a wave.

Will stood for a moment until it dawned on him.

13

The Reverend was standing at the gate with a smile. "I think you owe me a fiver."

"You're right, I do," Will laughed. "How about I give it to you next year?"

"It's a date," said the Reverend, popping his hat on.

iThink 2

"Oh, there's an ebubble from Zander," said Star. "I wonder what she wants. I just spoke to her on Hologram Skype."

"Hologram Skype. You're so old-fashioned Mum."

"You know I can't use that virtual multiverse machine. I love my old Hologram Skype portal. I don't know what I'll do when it vaporises. You can't get them anymore. Not even second hand on Spacebay. I wonder what Zander wants now."

"Well, why don't you pop the ebubble and find out?" said Star's son, tutting and throwing his eyes up to Vector Delta.

Star tipped the bubble above her head and heard her friend's voice say,

"Hi Star. Thanks for your ebubble. I'm sorry you don't like my suggestion of going to the Build a Boyfriend store to find a partner for the Cyber Ball. I just wish you'd told me when we were chatting on Hologram Skype. Rather than saying you thought it was a good idea, then ebubbling me later to say you thought it was a bad idea. I'm going ahead with it anyway. I hope I have more success than you expect."

Star stood with her mouth open, shaking her head at her son.

"Oooooh Mum," he said. "That must sting."

"I never sent that ebubble," said Star, still shaking her head. "I never sent it, and I would NEVER say that. I mean I thought it yeah, but I'd never say it."

Star heard her son stifle a triumphant, "Yes!"

"What are you up to?"

"Nothing!" he replied.

15

Star wasn't convinced. She knew to be suspicious when he had one of those 'Botox wouldn't melt' facial expressions.

"What have you done?" Star demanded. "Nova Cosmo Jeckyl! If I have to power your father up, I will."

Nova couldn't hold it in. "It worked," he squealed.

"What are you talking about? What worked?"

"iThink 2!"

"What is iThink 2?"

"It's my project for school, Mum. If you have a conversation with someone but you don't tell them everything that was in your head, it sends them an ebubble with all the words you thought but didn't say."

Star opened her mouth to shout at Nova, but nothing came out.

"You did say I could use your ebubble account for my project, Mum."

Star closed her mouth and opened it again.

"I'm gonna be famous." Nova strutted up and down the room. "When will dad be fully charged? I can't wait to tell him."

His mother's face turned from red to white and back to red.

"Are you okay Mum?" asked Nova. "Hey look, you just sent me 20 ebubbles."

The Rose Bowl

(Longlisted in the Penguin/RTÉ Guide Short Story Competition 2014)

Roseanna Mullan swept the tablecloth for non-existent creases and crumbs, moving the serving spoons half a centimetre one way, then the other, then back again. She stood back examining the symmetry of the place settings, moving to a different position to look again. When everything was ready she took the rose bowl from the cabinet and placed it in the centre of the table.

"The perfect hostess, as usual Roseanna darling. Why don't you go and get changed? The kids will be here soon."

"Robert, please make sure your golf clubs are in the car or the shed, and your newspapers are not all over the coffee table." Roseanna did another round of the table, eyeing the bowl from every angle before leaving the room.

Robert looked at the bowl in the centre of the table. It was the size of a small fruit bowl, pale pink in colour with ruby red rose buds that had gold-leaf stems, every inch or so around the outside. The rim at the top curved in and out, and was gilt edged. Robert thought about how often he'd looked at it as a child, knowing from a very young age it would be his.

His mother told him the story of its origins; or as much as she knew anyhow.

The bowl had been given to an ancestor and had passed down the family following the one strange stipulation given by the original owner centuries ago. It had to be passed from father to daughter to her son, then to his daughter and so forth. Not until the 21st Century, and the Mullans, were the terms unable to be fulfilled. A welcome clause in the legacy stated that if a daughter should be next to receive the bowl, but there was no daughter to leave it to, the eldest son could inherit providing any living siblings agreed, and legal papers were signed by all parties. Robert had wanted to do it years ago when their third boy was born. He arrived after the anguish of a miscarried baby girl, and neither Robert nor Roseanna could bring themselves to deal with writing a will, despite the urging of the American lawyers in whose hands lay the responsibility of the legacy.

At the announcement that their first grandchild was on the way, Robert and Roseanna arranged a meeting. Robert felt it was a serendipitous opportunity to arrange where the rose bowl would end up next. His mother often remarked that the bowl itself always decided its own fate.

An hour later six people were seated for lunch. Robert and Roseanna were joined by their three sons: Barry, their eldest, Ray, and their youngest, Cal. The sixth guest was Barry's wife Zahreena. A beautiful, rich, educated Iranian woman, who had agreed to wed Barry just eight weeks after meeting him.

Roseanna scowled across the table as Cal told Zahreena about a friend who had met an Iranian girl on a plane once and her name was Kohinoor. The guy asked her to join him for dinner that night and she agreed. So he took her to his favourite Indian restaurant called the Koh-i-noor. The guy had thought it would be hilarious, but the girl didn't find it funny at all and refused to eat there. Robert had to stop himself from spitting his lunch all over the beautifully laid table; he thought it was hilarious too. The sight of his wife's face was enough to quash his laughter, as she called to her "idiot" son, telling him to stop talking rubbish. Earlier she had specifically warned him to keep his mouth shut at lunch. Robert thought she'd have known better at this stage.

Cal caught his mother's eye and winked. "Lovely foodage Rosie. Got any bread I can dip into this gravy?" he asked, licking his fingers, to his mother's outrage.

Ray, the middle Mullan boy, was quiet, watching everything that was going on. Zahreena was a thing of glistening beauty and he winced inside every time he saw her touch Barry's hand or smile at his comments. He knew his brother had no idea of the jewel he had married, or how lucky he was.

"Alright everyone," said Robert, tapping his glass with a fork. "We need to call this thing to order. When we organised this little get together there was some family business to sort out, but now it has turned into a celebration. Zahreena and Barry, congratulations on your news. We wish you every happiness for the future."

"Hear hear," shouted Cal as he refilled his glass, splashing wine on the table cloth, and Zahreena's untouched dessert.

Zahreena nodded and smiled; she and Barry leaned in for a kiss and there was more cheering and jeering from Cal.

"I apologise Zahreena, but we do have to deal with this legal thing. Do you mind if we get it out of the way and then we can have all the baby talk in the world?"

"That is quite all right Robert, you must continue your business."

"Thank you Zahreena. Well boys, as you know I didn't want to put it off any longer. I want to amend my will to reflect what will happen to the rose bowl."

They all breathed, and paused for a moment, looking at the priceless glass bowl in the centre of the table. Everyone in the family was besotted by it. It was as if it held a gentle power over them. Robert Mullan was glad that the terms of the legacy meant it did not have to leave their home until they both died; but they had to deal with the fact that they had no daughter to leave it to.

"So, boys, we need to talk about my will. The lawyers from Maurice, Dalton and Basick will be here shortly to sign the papers. It'll be good to get this over with and done."

"I bet Bar can't wait to get his hands on *the precious*." Cal refilled his glass while doing his commonplace Gollum impression. "How much will you get on eBay for it Barry?"

"You know bloody well he can't sell it on eBay or anywhere else Calum Mullan. Now be quiet, and sober up while you're at it."

19

Roseanna said this while walking to Cal's chair, grabbing the bottle of wine from his hand.

"Sorry mammy, I know I'm an inconvenience. What a shame you NEED me to sign those papers, otherwise you could have had your little soirée without me."

Roseanna ignored him trying to swallow her anger, if only for Zahreena's sake. She was more than a little intimidated by the pedigree of her daughter-in-law and never felt relaxed in her company.

"Okay that's enough from you Cal. I emailed you all copies of the file. I'm presuming the lack of response meant it's okay? The lawyers will be coming here in about an hour, we can get this thing signed and I can put the bowl back in my display cabinet where it belongs."

Ray spoke for the first time. "What if we didn't agree?"

Everything stopped, even Cal's Gollum impressions.

"What do you mean?"

"Well, what if I decided that I didn't agree Barry should have it?"

"What's wrong, Ray? Jealous that Bar has all the jewels and you have none?" Cal snorted a laugh and Ray ignored him.

"It would mean court battles and long legal nonsense that would cost us a fortune, that's what. Is there a problem Ray?" Robert Mullan answered the question himself with the look he gave Ray.

"No, just curious Dad. Was kinda surprised Cal didn't put up more of a fight, just to be an ass! I'm wondering what would have happened if he did." Ray and Cal exchanged a few expletives, then Ray retreated to silence.

"One last thing, and the most important thing. No one has told anyone about this or that the lawyers are coming here today? They were very serious about the privacy of this arrangement."

Once again everyone reassured Robert no one knew what was going on in the house that day, or who was coming. Robert couldn't help feeling what a burden the rose bowl had turned out to be; he admired his mother and their ancestors for dealing with her stewardship of it so well. He was ready for this legal stuff to be over.

In the living room, Zahreena and Roseanna talked babies, nurseries and private hospitals. Zahreena had dropped the bombshell that she would go home to Tehran to have the baby. Roseanna was devastated, but was hiding it well. While their conversation went on Cal was tucking into the brandy, Robert was talking business to Barry, who was trying desperately to keep up; and Ray had gone outside to make a phone call.

The lawyers arrived soon after. After some introductions, Zahreena excused herself to give the family some privacy. She offered to go outside and send Ray in to sign the papers.

Zahreena walked the outskirts of the large garden in search of Ray. She was glad of the peace and sunlight of the afternoon. Glad too, this would soon be over, and the future of the rose bowl would be secure.

Near the end of the garden Zahreena felt a sudden pull on her arm. She let out a scream, but it was swallowed by a rough kiss on her mouth. She pushed against her assailant, but within seconds she was responding. When eventually Ray let go of her arm she slapped his face.

"You frightened me, you stupid fool of a man! What if someone had heard me scream?"

Ray grabbed her again and pushed against her.

"No, no. Not here. I am not a woman you can take in your garden. We will meet as planned on Tuesday night when Barry goes with your father to the board meeting."

"I hate this. I HATE IT. How did you talk me into this Zahreena? To marry him, and now have his child? If it even IS his child. It's more than I can bear – and all for what? That stupid bowl! It's too much. I want you back."

"Listen to me *Joon-am*. You know that for my family's honour I must once again own the rose bowl and it must be legal and binding.

21

My children are the rightful heirs of this treasure. Once my child is born I will take the bowl as my possession and we will be together."

Ray did not hear her. He slid to the ground with a low moan as the life drained from his body along with his blood. Zahreena stared at the man holding the blood-stained dagger.

"Farsham, why did you kill him here? You are reckless. It was to happen in the house with the others."

"He hurt you, pushing against you like you were a commoner. Let's go, the plane is waiting."

Zahreena followed her brother to a waiting car. Inside it her other three brothers sat, one holding the signed papers and a black velvet case with a golden clasp.

"Show me," Zahreena said.

He lifted the lid, and perfectly nestled in its red velvet setting was the rose bowl. "You have done great honour to our ancestors Zahreena. What is ours has been returned to us."

Zahreena nodded as the car pulled away without a sound.

The Last Days of Gertrude Hopkins

Everyone on the factory floor was delighted to hear the news that Gertrude Hopkins had handed in her notice. It was a great lift to the post-holiday blues January always brought. The staff were careful to celebrate quietly; any hint they were rejoicing would have brought more of her wrath. She'd be gone by the end of February, but she could still make life miserable in that time. Leap years usually only vaguely interested most people, but they damned the 29th of February that year. An extra day before they'd be shot of her.

Lunchtime was the best opportunity to talk about her; she never ate with them. She went out every day for lunch. No one knew where.

The theories of her reasons for leaving were discussed at great length. Many thought it was because of the announcement of new owners taking over the factory. Gertrude was the owner's niece, and her uncle had a lot to put up with. Most believed she knew no other boss would stand for her terrible attitude and work practices. She was jumping before she was pushed.

One person suggested she was getting married, but that was dismissed immediately. Maybe she was moving to some exotic clime, but no one could imagine her in a sunhat with an umbrella drink. Every day the theories rolled around, but it didn't matter why. The good news was she was going.

Wendy suggested a card and a collection, as was the custom when people were leaving. But no one wanted to sign it or give money to such a dragon. Wendy felt bad for Gertrude, but she was outvoted and shouted down. She inwardly thought she might send a card herself on the QT.

There would be no goodbye drinks do, either. Gertrude wouldn't turn up anyway.

"Doesn't mean we can't have a celebration." Frank the cleaner offered the suggestion.

There was a moment of silence and then a cheer for a night out to celebrate the goodbye (and good riddance) to Gertrude Hopkins.

Gertrude knew everything that was going on. She rarely left the building for lunch. Well, she left, but then she always let herself back in via a service door. She would sit eating her lunch listening to their conversations. That day, she listened to them discuss the celebration of her departure and felt sad for the first time. She knew she was not liked, but she really didn't think they would be THAT happy she was moving on. She had thought she would miss this, listening to all their chatter and gossip, but hearing their joy and plans of a night out turned her sadness back to anger. She decided not to bother listening any more. For her last few days as floor manager, she would treat herself to lunch out.

The next day at lunch time, Wendy braved the question again.

"I ... I ... I really think we should invite her."

There was a collective "WHAT?"

"Well, you said it yourself. She won't come, but it would be nice to ask her. We can't have a goodbye do for her and not invite her. I won't enjoy it. I'll feel bad. It'll be like we're mocking her, and I ... well, I just don't want to do that."

No one said much that day, but the next day at lunch, one of the older men who had worked there even longer than Gertrude said Wendy's words from the previous day had stayed with him, and maybe she was right. There were only four days to go until the arranged night out, and a few people around the tables needed convincing. But on Gertrude's second-last day, it was agreed Wendy should approach her and invite her.

Gertrude was her usual frosty self, but Wendy was determined, and with a quiet confidence asked Gertrude if she would like to go out for a drink the following night. Just a little get-together to wish her well as she moved on. Gertrude was shocked but hid it well with nonchalance. She snipped that it was very late notice but she didn't have anything on and would see them there.

Wendy was thrilled and went back to the group with the good news. To her it was good news, anyway.

Gertrude had no intention of turning up, as obviously they had a plan to humiliate her, and there was no way she was going to give them the last laugh. She was determined to have that.

On Gertrude's last day, she was delightful to everyone. She greeted all the staff individually. She was helpful, smiling, pleasant and patient. Some thought it was terrifying, most just thought it was weird. Her team were kind of chuffed with themselves, though; it seemed their invitation had melted her heart. Wendy was sad they hadn't made the effort earlier, but she was so delighted things were going to end well.

In the pub that night, Wendy put up a little poster saying goodbye to Gertrude. Others brought some snacks, and a last-minute collection had been taken and a small gift bought.

Time passed, but there was no sign of Gertrude. The nibbles were eaten, and at some stage the poster was ripped off the wall. They were all disgusted, and after a few drinks, even Wendy was vocal about how she'd give Gertrude a piece of her mind if she ever saw her again.

When another round of drinks was ordered, the barman asked if the group gathered were the mystery lottery winners. He said that someone local won the lottery jackpot last month and had just gone public. They hadn't heard. Frank the cleaner, their usual source of local news, hadn't even opened his paper with all the busyness of the day. He dug it out of his overcoat pocket and, after looking at the front page, threw the paper down on the table in front of him, pointing, unable to speak.

The headline read, *'Local Lottery Winner Gertrude Hopkins buys family business and will assume role of Managing Director from March 1st.'*

Blessed Assurance
(Winner of Newbridge Junefest 2014)

There are moments that stop you. I didn't know everything there was to know about my mother, but I also didn't think that nine years after her death, she could shock me into stillness and silence. Blunt grief is sharpened again as I look at her signature; a scrawl that is both illegible and unmistakable.

The page is mostly yellow, around the edges almost brown, with faded letters, punched by a real typewriter. There is a perfect patch in the middle; a little section of this outsized, almost parchment-like document that has kept its original soft cream colour. It has been protected from the corrosion of light and time.

I wipe my face to stop a salty tear from damaging the insurance policy.

Name of Assured: Elizabeth Hyland
Name of the Life Assured: Annie Hyland
Relationship to Life Assured: Mother
Date of policy: 06 11 1971
Age Next Birthday: 1 year
Monthly Premium: £0.30
Amount Payable: £36

I search my memory for any remnants of a conversation about this, but there is nothing there. She may well have taken the time to explain it all to me; I spent a lot of time pretending to listen. So many things I forget about her. I have pieces of connection with her, snippets of conversations I wasn't fully engaged in and that I ended as quickly as I could, to go and do something cooler than talk to my mother.

The yellow page is one of a bundle that spilled out of a torn envelope, as I emptied her wardrobe. There is one of these large yellow sheets for six of her eight children. Some must have gone missing; she wouldn't have left anyone out. There are two for some of us, including me; and six for my father.

My mother had little. She had eight children, two jobs, and a husband who worked 14 hours a day; but she didn't have much to show for the hard graft their life was. I look again at the policies and wonder how she was able to pay each month; correction, most months. We hid behind the sofa from the knock at the door, like a lot of families in those days. As kids we thought it was funny, but she must have been panicking.

I remember her stressing, each meal time. I would look wide-eyed at the steaming mashed potato piled high on my father's plate; and draped over it, two slices of corned beef.

"Bring that in to your Da," she would sigh, trying to share out the spoonful of potato left in the pot between the rest of us. I've no idea what she had for her dinner.

I'm not sure how it happened, but my father came from a household where there was a little bit of dessert every day. After dinner, dad was presented with tea and a slice of bread and jam; the best my mother could do. If you were lucky enough to be asked to carry it in, you could accidentally catch some jam on your finger to savour on the way back.

I wonder why she paid the insistent sales man the 30 pence, plus 25 pence, plus 14 pence, plus 45 pence, plus 12 pence, plus, plus, plus … it all adds up when you've nothing to spare.

In some ways, the insurance sales patter is the same today as it has always been; focusing on the 'what if?' What if your phone was stolen or you dropped it after the warranty ran out? Those questions appeal to little more than my vanity and I always ignore them.

In my mother's day however, those questions appealed to fear.

"Oh your boy is sick? Ahh Missus, I'm sorry to hear that. Please God now he'll be grand, because the cost of a funeral these days is a mortal sin. Do you know what you should do ...?"

"Wasn't that a terrible accident up there in the factory? I tell you, now that she's lost her oul' fella I don't know what she'll do. If only she'd taken one of these policies ..."

So, she exchanged the worry of what might happen for the worry of a payment she was rarely able to make without suffering herself.

I carefully fold the awkward pages back into their familiar creases and though they really should go into a better envelope, I can't bring myself to throw out the torn one.

Another glance at my mother's signature seals in me a new level of loss and admiration.

Finished

"Why don't you drink the last mouthful of your tea?"

"Huh?" Her husband didn't look up.

"The last mouthful, why do you always leave it?" She swilled the cup out in the sink.

"Dunno," he said, chewing his pen.

"You never finish anything," she said, rattling the cups in the sudsy water.

"What?" He put the crossword down.

"Well you don't." She kept her back to him. "The garden project, sorting out the spare room ..." She slammed cutlery on the draining board. "You put that awful monstrosity in the hall. It's been there two years, half of it sanded and the other half as mucky as ever."

"*That* monstrosity was my father's bureau."

"And even the tea I make you – you never finish it."

After a minute of silence, except for the dishes going back in the cupboard, he spoke.

"Leaves."

"What?"

"Leaves," he said. "Tea leaves. I don't want to swallow them, so I *leave* them in the cup." He would have smiled at his fabulous joke had he not still been smarting over the bureau comment.

"I don't use tea leaves."

"I know that, but it's a habit. I never ever used to drink the last mouthful at home. My mother always used real tea leaves. She taught me not to empty the cup, so I wouldn't end up with a mouthful. It's just an old childhood tradition."

The mention of his mother made bile rise in her throat. She closed the cupboard and opened the fridge. "Pork chops do you for dinner?"

31

"I suppose they'll have to," he said from behind his paper.

She began peeling potatoes.

"I'm going to have a go at that bureau, since you're getting so worried about it. I'm giving up on this," he said, waving the paper at her.

After he left the room, she walked over to the table. She picked up the paper and read the one clue left unsolved.

12 down. The longest sentence, just for two. (1, 2)

She picked up the pen and wrote 'I DO', before going back to peeling the potatoes.

First Dance
(First Published NFFD Flashflood 2017)

Of all the things she was nervous about, the first dance worried her more than anything. She wasn't sure why it affected her beyond any other part of the wedding preparation. Maybe it was because the song itself spoke exactly of how she felt.

The death of her dad earlier that year meant the job of giving his daughter away would have to go to her brother. She knew her mother would be proud and tearful, and with the cousins coming home from Canada, it was going to be wonderful.

There was so much to do in the run-up to the big day that she was able to stay busy and occupied. When it came to practicalities, she was an expert. The flowers, the cake, even the dress … none of it made her emotional. She was in organisation mode and had her 'management hat' on, protecting not just her head, but her heart too. Every so often, talk of the reception would pull her thoughts back to the dance, and she knew as soon as that song, their song, started, she would not be able to hold back the tears. She wondered if it would be better to just let herself cry.

The day of the wedding started with torrential rain, but nothing dampened the spirits. As the hairdresser fixed the tiny white flowers in her hair, she chatted away to the bridal party. The sparkling white wine helped to add to the air of cheer as family and friends gathered to watch the beautiful bride get into the car with her brother.

Photos were taken at every stage, from every angle. She wanted the photographer to capture every smile, she just hoped her tears would not be one of the everlasting images of this wonderful day. Everything was indeed wonderful - all a bride and a family could ask for on a wedding day. Even the rain stopped, and the sun came out for the photos. The meal was fabulous and the service by hotel staff impeccable. She was having a tremendous day and almost forgot how nervous she had been. After dinner, when they left the room to let the band set up, her heart started to pound. She knew now that she could do nothing to stop the tears. This wedding had been eighteen months in the planning, and the thought of the first dance was the thing that consistently gave her a lump in her throat.

Everyone gathered around the dance floor and waited for the bride and groom to take to the floor. As the opening chords of their song struck up, she gritted her teeth and pasted on her smile. The sparkling couple walked to the middle of the floor to the rapturous applause of their family and friends.

"How could you not cry at a moment like this?" she thought, as she watched her sister, her best friend, dance with the man she herself had always loved.

The Total Eclipse of Little Freddie

Little Freddie was, well, little. She stood a dinky four foot eleven to my box-like five foot four, but I always felt in the shadow of Little Freddie when I stood next to her. Her olive skin gave her a beautiful warm glow. So not only was I gargantuan next to her, I was pasty.

Little Freddie's stature was the only small thing about her. Her personality filled any space she inhabited in the way her stature never would. Her laugh resounded around the room. Not in a grating way that makes you turn your head and tut. It was a laugh that cheered, like sun after a cloud passed; not blinding your eyes, just warming your face. Her heart though; it was her heart that outshone everything else. Her generosity didn't come from guilt or burden; the kind that announces itself with faux humility and exaggerated self-deprecation. No, Freddie's kindness was subtle, gentle, quiet, and constant.

There was only one occasion I ever overshadowed her, and it was the day we met. I was on a bus. I took up three quarters of the seat, as usual, and Freddie came to sit beside me, taking up less than the remaining space. People usually don't sit beside me. There isn't the room. But there we were on the bus to Aberderi, perfectly proportioned; as we have been ever since.

I was engrossed in my book and didn't hear the driver say there was an incident ahead and we'd be stopping. When everyone got up to go, Little Freddie gently tapped my arm. "We're all off here love," she said.

I had no idea where I was, but I knew this wasn't Aberderi. The instructions barked at me over the phone were to get the Aberderi bus and not to get off until the last stop. I had no number to make contact and no wish to do so.

"Where are we?" I stammered.

Little Freddie squeezed my arm. "Llandaran. Only about twenty minutes short of Bargoed, but we have to stop because of an accident up ahead."

Two ladies called the stop a blessing and scuttled off to find a place they could 'make themselves comfortable for the rest of the journey'. The one man on the bus had a brief chat with the driver then disappeared into a pub.

"What now, Drive?" Little Freddie looked up at the young man who seemed more lost than I was.

"I'm not sure. We can't get through is all I know. We've to stay put until my supervisor arrives."

The apologetic tone seemed to appeal to Freddie and she comforted him, encouraging him that it was not his fault and he had acted responsibly in doing as he was instructed. She thought he might even be awarded some accolade for what seemed to me to be the standard obedience of a company lackey.

"So, what will we do now?" Little Freddie asked.

I was stumped, with no idea what to do next. "I need to get to Aberderi," I said.

Little Freddie smiled at me. "None of us is going to Aberderi now love; not for a while. Will we go for a cup of tea?"

It was the last thing I wanted but I couldn't come up with a reason not to. Into the little café we went; leaving the bus driver looking up and down the road willing a solution out of thin air.

The tea shop was small and in the not so far corner, the two other ladies from the bus were both talking at the same time, something about pillow cases. Little Freddie insisted on paying and soon we were sat with tea and a toasted tea cake each.

Freddie talked non-stop for the next hour – she asked me several questions about my life and family and I even got to answer a few. She gave me her life history and that of a number of people she was related to. How such a tiny person fitted so much in, I'm not sure, but she had a full life.

In one of my brief contributions to the conversation, I revealed that I love to read. She insisted we take a walk to the little second-hand book shop down the street, and she dashed out ahead of me. The bus driver was standing in the same spot as we passed him. Freddie patted him on the arm and made some maternal noises as she whizzed by him.

We went left, right, left and left again. Freddie suddenly stopped in the middle of a row of terraced houses and let herself in with the key that was in the door. The sitting room was full of overcrowded bookshelves. There was a basket on the sideboard, with a few coins in it, and the sound of Radio Cymru drifted in from a distant room. Little Freddie was silent for the first time since the bus had stopped. She was lost in wonder as she looked around the tiny room. I found one or two books I liked. A tatty copy of a collection of Dylan Thomas poems and copy of *1984* that looked like it had never even been opened. I dropped some money in the basket, and we let ourselves out and walked back towards the main street.

Progress and action were evident when we got there.

A trailer bearing a mangled car was parked on the street, a tow truck was pulling a slightly less mangled tractor.

It seemed that, miraculously, no one had been hurt. The rescue mission had been complicated by the narrow road and a herd of sheep being brought from one field to another.

The passengers all appeared out of their watering holes just as we got to the bus, where the driver stood with a cautious smile.

Freddie dashed back into the tea shop we'd been in, lamenting she hadn't thanked the lady who had served us. She called to the driver she'd be right back, which seemed to put an end to his attempts at happiness.

The rest of us got on the bus and as I took my seat I looked at the tractor on the tow truck. Two men in deep conversation stood with their backs to the truck, one drawing pictures in the air with his hand as he told his story. At first, I thought the bus was starting to move and jumped up to remind the driver about Freddie. As I got to him I realised the bus had not moved. It was the trailer that was moving, slow at first, picking up speed as it came down the hill.

Freddie came out of the tea shop. She was still talking and waving to the owner as she backed out. I saw her look up when it went dark. She was looking to see the cloud that had covered the sun. It wasn't a cloud.

I wish I could say that bravery and gallantry made me run. When I think of what I did, I shudder. I didn't decide to save Freddie's life. I was propelled by something behind me that sent a flame up my legs and pushed me off the bus. She hadn't seen the truck until that moment. She turned to face me as I lunged towards her. Her face contorted, I pushed her, and we fell in a heap as the draught of the passing trailer chilled us further.

For a moment there was silence. The leaves were still, the birds had forgotten how to sing. Then a flurry of noise and movement. It took a moment before I was sure we were both still alive. With help, I moved off Freddie. She was pale, her mouth open, but no words came out. We were led into the tea shop to wait for help. Freddie's head was bleeding and the palms of my hands were studded with tarmac and glass. Other than that, neither of us had any injuries. Paramedics insisted on taking us to hospital, though we both protested.

We went in separate ambulances and I had thought, to separate hospitals, until Little Freddie's gurney was wheeled next to mine.

I was embarrassed but glad to see her.

"How does it feel?" she asked me, after a while.

"Sore," I said waving my bandaged hands.

"No," she said. "How does it feel to be a hero?"

"I'm no hero," I said, wishing I could run away. "You'd have been better off if I'd left you. I hit your head off the ground."

"Yes, but I stood up because of you, love."

We sat in quiet and I swallowed hard, staring at the wall. Freddie placed her small hand on my bandaged one and I watched my tears make grey circles on the white sheet.

38

I was glad when the policeman arrived. He asked lots of questions, which neither of us answered very well. He asked us if there was anyone we wanted to call.

We both answered no at the same time.

"No partners, children? No relatives I can call?" the policeman's investigation was not over.

Freddie turned to me. "What about your visit to Aberderi?"

"I was going to a funeral. I didn't really know her, but I felt I had to go."

"No friends, not one?" The policeman seemed eager to hand me over.

"No," I said. "I've no friends, not anywhere near here. I've no one really."

I'd never said that out loud before. It was sharp.

"You do have someone," said Freddie. "You'll always have someone now."

True to her word, Little Freddie has been my friend for many years. Always sharing her light with me; never again giving me the opportunity to eclipse her.

The End of the Alphabet Kids

Alison Abraham and Brandon Bryans wanted twenty-six children. They thought it would be fun to have a troop of children, each one with a name beginning with a different letter of the alphabet. When their first daughter was born they were going to start the process by calling her Alison, but reconsidered, starting with the other end of the alphabet.

Baby Zara Abraham-Bryans brought more joy to their lives than they ever imagined possible and when she was six months old they found out they were expecting number two. Yolanda was seven weeks premature and at one stage they thought she wouldn't make it; but the little fighter was soon growing and making as much noise as her big sister.

Once Yolanda was thriving, thoughts turned to baby number three. Fourteen months later Xavier James was born.

Life in the Abraham-Bryans household functioned like a production line. There was an excellent system that kept bottles washed, sterilised and filled for the next feed. Alison had dreams of saving the planet along with having a large number of children, but when Xavier was born she knew it was unrealistic and reluctantly went over to disposable nappies. The washing of clothes, vests, baby bed sheets and bibs was more than enough to keep up with.

On Xavier's first birthday the house was full to bursting with babies and toddlers and the questions every other mum wanted answers to were: when would Alison be pregnant again, and what they would call the baby?

Alison's friend Sally was feeding her own new-born. "W isn't a great letter is it? It's not much easier than the others."

"You think? I mean they could have Will, Walt, Warren ... uh ..." Brandon's sister Barbara was stuck.

"See what I mean? Warren? Walter? Not great names. And if they have a girl you've got Wendy and Whitney. I mean I don't think they've thought ..."

Barbara nudged Sally as Alison came back in the room.

"You okay Ali?"

"Yeah, all good. Couldn't find the matches, and now that I have, the candles have disappeared."

Alison was throwing stuff, moving toys from one chair to another. Every so often stopping to sigh and then starting her vain search again.

Eventually both the matches and candles were found. Happy Birthday was sung enough times so every child could blow the candles out. Babies were asleep in prams and toddlers were almost asleep on bean bags in front of the TV showing *Monsters Inc*. The mums surveyed the mess, ignored it and opened another bottle of wine.

All this time the dads had been out in the garden. Once or twice one ventured in to check if any help was needed but backed away slowly returning to the safety of the children who'd decided to play football.

They too discussed the expected announcement of baby W; in Brandon's absence of course. Less concerned with the name and more concerned with the fact that the more children Brandon had, the less he looked like he had the energy to make another one.

It was after midnight before Brandon and Alison collapsed into bed. Zara and Yolanda were very lively due to the unusually high blood sugar levels, so it was almost 10pm before all three children were sound asleep. Then the mountains of paper cups and plates were collected from every corner and surface, lumps of goodness-only-knew what were scraped off tables and walls, and spillages were mopped up.

They lay on top of the bedclothes still fully dressed.

"None of the girls asked if I was pregnant again. First time since I had Xavier's christening. Did the guys mention it?"

42

"Nope," Brandon said through a yawn.

After about five minutes Brandon had a miraculous revival and felt like he might just have some energy left after all.

"Hey, honey."

Alison wanted to cry.

"Oh Brandon, please. I'm exhausted. And anyway, I think it's too soon."

"Awh honey." The wounded voice. "It's not too soon. Don't you think we've left it long enough?"

"No Brandon I don't." Alison sat up. "I spoke to the doctor when I brought Yolanda in for her check-up. He said we should leave it another couple of weeks."

"Honey that *was* two weeks ago."

"Nooooo. Really?"

"Yep. It's been eight weeks since my vasectomy. I'm good to go."

Leaving Sarah

Marian stood at the bedroom window surveying the damage. The sun was shining almost white in a clear sky; the garden furniture on its side and flooded pot plants assured her last night's storm was real. She was about to turn away from the window when she spotted it. It looked like a pile of clothes in the corner of the garden. She considered going out to tidy it up but there were so many other things that needed to be done.

When Marian looked again, the pile of clothes had moved, and she thought she saw a face. She quickly dressed and ran, tripping over the suitcase on the landing; swearing at it all the way down the stairs. She looked through the kitchen window, the pile of clothes had moved again.

Marian caught her breath as she saw the shape form and a hand emerge from the pile. She found herself at the bottom of the garden; the pile of clothes was still again, and the hand had disappeared. Marian wondered if she'd imagined it. The nearer she got to it, the more it looked like nothing.

"Is there someone there?"

"Please help." The pile of clothes spoke so quietly Marian almost missed it.

"Did you say something? Who's there?"

"Please … please, help!" The quiet cry came again. Marian took a step back at the young female voice.

"Who are you? What are you doing here?"

The clothes moved, and a teenage girl appeared. She had long hair that was soaking wet. The coats covering her were all saturated. She was clutching a plastic bag stuffed with newspapers.

45

"Help! Please, I think she's dead." The young girl offered the plastic bag, and Marian saw the tiny face surrounded by wet newspaper.

She grabbed the bag and ran, reaching the house by the time the mother had found the energy to cry out. She ran warm water in the kitchen sink and taking the newspapers off the baby, gently laid her into it. The baby opened her eyes, made a little noise then closed her eyes again as the warm water surrounded her.

"You're perfect – you little precious; you're perfect." Marian's heart was racing as she rubbed the baby's skin with warm water.

The mother was now lying across the threshold of the back door. "Is she alive?"

Marian concentrated on the baby. As she warmed up she began to cry, with the same weakness her mother had spoken. Marian grabbed a couple of tea towels and wrapped the baby. She looked properly at the mother for the first time, who was now huddled in a ball on the kitchen floor.

Marian closed the door and wrapped the baby in a blanket she had draped over the back of her sofa. She boiled some milk and tried to get it into the baby with a teaspoon.

"You need to get out of those wet clothes. I'll run a bath for you. You need to go to the hospital. So does this little one."

"NO! No hospitals. I just need to sleep."

"You need to get out of those clothes or you'll die of pneumonia. I'm going to run a bath for you."

Marian took the baby and went upstairs, careful to manoeuvre around the suitcase this time. The other suitcase was open on the bed. She took some of the clothes out of it and put the baby into it. While the bath was running she went into the spare room. She grabbed a bag marked 'Charity Shop' and ripped it open. She found some clothes and went into the bathroom to turn the taps off. She checked the baby then went downstairs.

The mother was in the same position as when she'd left her.

"Come on, have a bath, put some dry clothes on and we'll see what to do next. What's your name?"

"Sarah."

"What's the baby's name?"

"I don't know."

*****

Marian was heating soup on the cooker. "You two need to see a doctor! When did you have her?"

"I don't know."

"How did you cut the cord Sarah?"

"I don't know."

"How did you get into my garden?"

"I don't know I DON'T KNOW. STOP ASKING ME QUESTIONS!"

It was the loudest Sarah had spoken. The baby opened her eyes for just a second at the sound of her mother's voice.

"Here, have this."

Sarah dipped bread into the soup in slow motion and ate a little. Soon she was asleep again.

What do I do now? thought Marian. She had no one she could call. There was nobody left.

She thought about the hospital, but she couldn't take the chance. She could never get there herself, and if she rang for an ambulance, her social worker would be here before it arrived. She didn't want social services back in her life. Marian looked up at the mantelpiece above the fire to a picture of two little girls.

"Sarah, wake up! We need to talk. I'm moving out of this house tomorrow. You need to decide what you're going to do."

Sarah lifted her head. "Can I lie on your sofa?"

Marian nodded.

Sarah walked over to the sofa and sat down. She looked up at the photo.

"Who are they?"

"It doesn't matter who they are!" Marian snapped. "Have you someone I can call? Family or a friend?"

"No."

"Maybe I can get you into a shelter? You can't go back to sleeping rough. You'll never survive it, and neither will she."

"Are they your kids in that picture?"

"Yes."

"Where are they?"

Marian felt a sharp pain in her gut.

"I don't know. London, I think."

"Is that where you're going? To London, to see them?"

"Sarah, it doesn't matter where I'm going. Where are YOU going to go?"

"I don't know." Sarah rolled up in a ball again and started to rock gently.

Marian put her head in her hands and squeezed her eyes tightly shut hoping for inspiration.

*****

When Marian woke hours had passed. Sarah was still asleep, but the baby was starting to whimper. After giving her some boiled milk, she held her for a while and started to sing to her. She closed her eyes and wished that when she opened them she'd be looking at one of her own girls. Marian felt the blanket get suddenly warm, then wet. She laughed out loud. "You little monkey! I suppose it's a good sign." She cleaned her up and put a makeshift nappy on her. She felt bad, but knew if she went out and anyone saw her buying nappies they'd probably ring the police.

Laying the baby safely on the sofa she went to the hall. She picked up a bag marked 'Throw Away' and felt the pain again. She put it beside the sofa and ripped it open. As children's clothes spilled out, Marian's tears followed. She picked up each item and smelled it. She tried to find some clothes small enough for the baby but ended up holding every dress and cardigan close to her face. She found the two matching denim dresses with the girls' names embroidered on the back. *Aimee* and *Sophie*. She thought her heart might burst. She dressed the baby in the smallest thing she could find, and wept.

She carried the baby over to the photo of her daughters; their smiles always made her feel better. As she had done many times before, Marian looked at the faces of her children, told them how she loved them, how sorry she was for her terrible mistake and how much she regretted not fighting harder to keep them. She held the baby tighter, singing to her and rocking her until exhaustion took over and she sat down to sleep again.

*****

Marian looked at the baby in the suitcase. There was something wrong. The baby was crying; screaming. Why did she look like Sophie? This baby wasn't Sophie. Then she heard another cry. There was another suitcase and another baby. It was Aimee. It was all wrong. Both babies were screaming. Marian looked from one baby to the next, she tried to comfort them, but they wouldn't stop crying. She tried to reach for them, but someone was holding her back. She started to struggle, she kicked and pushed and pulled.

"Let me hold my children. They are my daughters, they need me. Let go of me. They are my children. LET GO OF ME…"

Marian woke with a jump and could hear a baby crying. In an instant she caught up with her reality.

"Sarah?"

Marian took the baby up.

"Sarah, you're going to have to go to the shop and get some nappies and some baby milk or something. I can't keep giving her the boiled stuff."

Marian went down the stairs calling Sarah's name.

Marian's handbag was on the kitchen counter; it was empty. Her phone, diary and keys were on the floor. Her purse was there, but it

49

was open, and the cash was gone. A couple of drawers in the kitchen were open but they were already empty. There had been nothing to take.

The photo of the twins was on the table with a scrap of paper underneath it. One word scrawled on it.

Sorry.

Marian searched the house and even checked the bottom of the garden. Sarah was gone. It was 10am before Marian even looked at her watch for the first time. She picked up her mobile phone and scrolled through the numbers. She hesitated at one or two, but she knew there was no one who would take her call.

The doorbell rang.

Sarah! Marian ran to the door. Through the glass she could see it wasn't her.

Did she recognise me? Oh God, did she call the police?

"HANG ON PLEASE!"

She put the baby safely in the sofa corner propped up by all the cushions.

A rep from a car hire firm was standing at the door. She had totally forgotten her rental car was being delivered.

He introduced himself and Marian waited for the flash of recognition to cross his face. He didn't flinch; he had no idea who she was.

The man walked around the car and Marian pretended to listen to what he was saying. He went on about the features of the car, what was in the boot, something about the glovebox and the stereo.

"Ms Redland? Errr … Ms Redland?"

"Yes, I'm so sorry. Yes, that's fine. Thank you."

"Great, and the car seat?"

"I'm sorry?"

"Well, as I said, there is a car seat in the boot, if you don't need it we can take it away to give you more room."

Everything stopped. It had not occurred to her before, but now ... well now it made total sense. She argued with herself for half a second, but she already knew what she was going to do.

She looked again at the man to make sure he hadn't recognised her. He was looking at her with a nervous smile.

"That's great. You can leave it. I don't need it at the moment but I'm visiting family and it may come in handy."

Lying had become so easy.

"Oh great! Well thank you, Ms Redland. And you have a safe trip now!"

*****

Marian drove for two hours in the opposite direction of her intended route. She knew there was a large superstore off the motorway in a retail park. The bigger and more off the beaten track the better. She was putting the shopping bags in the car when she heard a voice.

"They need twice as much stuff as we do, don't they?"

She swung around. "WHAT?"

The woman was embarrassed.

"Babies," the uneasy reply came. She nodded at the bags bulging with nappies, formula milk and baby wipes. "They don't travel light do they?" She ventured a nervous giggle.

"Oh sorry, yes, sorry." Marian laughed. It was genuine – it was relief. "Oh yes, far more than we do – for such small people."

They both laughed, and the awkwardness passed.

Both women continued to pack shopping into their cars.

Marian finished first, getting into the driver's seat she smiled at the fellow shopper.

"Goodbye now. Sarah, say bye bye to the nice lady."

The other woman looked into the car as it moved away, her smile dropping at the sight of an empty car seat.

Wishes on Stars

The closing credits rolled, and the theme tune opened with power chords that would bring a tear to a Guns'n'Roses fan. They watched her as she wrote with furious haste.

She was the most feared movie critic in Hollywood. Her words determined whether your premiere was attended by a cast of thousands of Hollywood's finest, or the cast of Star Trek.

Wishes Puddlestock!

The name struck fear in the heart of every movie producer and director; and quite a number of pretzel vendors.

The music ended, and house lights faded up. Most of the film critics were already sipping Mai Tais on Hollywood Boulevard, but not Wishes. Hunched over her pad, she jealously guarded her words as they poured onto the page like molasses on homemade ice cream.

"She's taking too long dammit." Ralph Ecclestein paced, knowing a long review from Wishes was bad. Her five-star reviews were always less than ten words.

"Someone make a note that I may need to call Leonard Nimoy's agent in the morning."

"Booking him for the premiere again boss?" Ecclestein's assistant ventured the question; but no coherent answer came. Just a series of grunts and muffled swears as Ecclestein continued doing laps of the viewing booth.

"She had her eyes closed for most of it, m-m-maybe that's a good sign?" The meek voice came from a dark corner of the room.

"What?" Ecclestein swung around. "Who the hell are you? What are you talking about? Who is this guy?"

"Boss! He's the new intern. What do you mean kid? What are you saying? Get over here!"

"Well … It's just … I noticed her close her eyes a lot. She was concentrating hard. Especially at that scene. You know, where the bad guy confesses his love for the gal who's about to have her appendix taken out by the other bad guy; the one pretending to be a surgeon?"

"That's the best scene of the whole damn movie!"

"Yeah, well she had her eyes closed for most of it."

"Dialogue!" Ecclestein punched the table. "Dammit! She was concentrating on the dialogue."

The discussion continued. Oblivious to it all, Wishes Puddlestock looked up and noticed the empty seats around her and blank screen in front of her. She put her pen down and took a deep breath. Moonlighting for Mills & Boon was taking its toll, but as usual she was able to complete a brand-new story in less than 120 minutes.

She'd already reworded the review she'd written for Ecclestein's previous movie. They were always the same anyway.

She put her pen and pad away and wondered if this should be her last review. Writing love stories was really all she ever wanted to do; maybe it was time to start doing it with the lights on. It felt like the right time to tell people that Wishes Puddlestock was putting down her pen and taking up … her other pen.

She headed for the door and waved at the viewing booth, stretching her fingers out to assure Ecclestein of his five stars.

He didn't see her, he was busy on the phone ordering flowers for George Takei.

The Bag Man

Michael left the science building by punching the door open with both fists. The security guard looked up and tutted, going straight back to his newspaper.

"This degree is more trouble than it's worth," he thought, stomping rather than walking through the campus towards the halls of residence. The earlier phone call did not help him prepare for the meeting he was dreading. He'd almost been able to put it out of his head while he was with his tutor, but now he'd have to deal with that too. He sat on his bed and fumed for a while, head in hands.

Reluctantly he stood to get changed. He hung his Diesel jeans and Jack & Jones shirt back in the wardrobe and pulled the tracksuit bottoms from the next hanger. He fought with them, refusing to get into them willingly and so lost his balance and ended up sitting on his bed. He reached for the cheap runners under the wardrobe and swapped them for the Converse he was wearing. Throwing on his fleece, he grabbed his baseball cap and an empty plastic bag hanging on the back of the door. On his way out, he passed one of his dorm mates.

"How did you get on, Mick?"

"It's a load of crap, Sam!" Michael said. "Honest to God, I'm this close to packing it in."

"No, man," said Sam grabbing Michael's shoulders.

Michael shook him off, but Sam grabbed him again.

"Mick! This is what you asked me to do when we were drunk the last night of Freshers'. You told me to grab you by the scruff of the neck and remind you that you said you were never going back. Never! I promised I would. Now here I am, keeping my promise. You have to keep your promise not to quit. Never to go back."

"I have to get my run in." Michael shrugged, and Sam let him go.

"Do your five miles, have a shower, and we'll go for a pint later yeah?" Sam put his hand out. Michael shook it then started to jog away. He didn't stop until he was out of the campus and at the bus stop.

The bus journey wasn't long enough. He'd have rather it took two hours to get into town. He argued with himself throughout the journey about college. He put his hands in his pockets and felt the plastic bag; it made him slump even further in the seat.

The sun made him squint as he walked up the quays. He hated not wearing his sunglasses, but he didn't want to risk anything happening to him. He headed up O'Connell Street and did his usual circuit of Parnell Square. No sign of anyone. He did the loop again and saw her, she was heading into the Garden of Remembrance with a man who looked twice her age.

He followed them in.

"There he is, me favourite. Alright Mikey?" The woman fell over, almost dropping her bottle.

"Howya Sal," Michael said, sitting down on the ground beside her. He handed her the empty plastic bag. "Here you go."

"Ah you're a star." Sal took off what was left of her shoe, put the bag over her foot and the shoe back on. "Them runners I bought you are lasting longer than these yokes," she said pointing at his feet.

"Who are you? What do you want? Get away from her!" Sal's companion was trying to punch the air near Michael's head.

"Shurrup Davey," said Sal, pushing him to join them on the ground.

"Sal, listen." Michael tried to eyeball her. "The social worker rang me this morning."

"Don't care."

"I know you don't care but the …"

"Don't care, don't care."

"Sal, you can't ignore …"

56

"Don't care, don't care, don't care, don't care, don't care, don't care!" Sal covered her ears and shook her head.

"LOOK YOU," Michael shouted. "I can't keep ..."

"You? YOU?" For just a second Sal was sobered by the hurt. She pushed herself away from Michael. "Don't call me YOU. You shouldn't even be using my name. You call me what you're supposed to call me. Go on. Who am I?"

"You're Sal, ye feckin' eejit." Davey was struggling to get back on his feet.

"Oh no," said Sal, keeping her eyes fixed on Michael. "Not to him."

Michael hated her pain. He stood up, straightened his clothes and sat down again.

"So tidy," said Sal. "Always so tidy. Even as a baby, you hated to be in a mess." She reached for his face, then took her hand back.

"Mam, please," Michael whispered.

Sal smiled, just a little. "Say it again."

Michael picked invisible fluff from his fleece.

"Mam."

Sal took a drink from her bottle and laid back on the ground. "Will we sleep here again tonight Davey? I like it here."

"And why not?" Davey lay down beside Sal.

Michael stood up and fixed his cap. He hesitated before walking away.

"I'll need another bag next week Mikey."

"I'm not coming back, Sal."

"Two bags, Mikey. They don't last like they used to when you got them for free."

Michael headed out on to the main street.

"Two bags Mikey, two bags son, two bags Mikey let's have another one!" Michael could hear Sal sing and Davey guffaw, then burst into a bout of coughing. He got his phone out and called Sam's number. It went to answerphone.

"Sam, mate, it's Mick. I'm sorry. You're right. Thanks man, thanks for reminding me. I'm on for that pint tonight if you are."

As he tucked the phone back in his fleece pocket, careful to close the zip, he could still hear Sal. She stayed in earshot all the way back to the bus stop, and long after he got back to his dorm room.

Cecile is Gone

The year is almost over and still no news of Cecile. It occurred to me again as I listened to the news headlines tell of far-off tragedies, she is most likely dead. Could Sandrita be so cruel? Could she know and not tell me? Maybe my Cecile, my only child, has perished and I do not know. Has Sandrita found something else to keep from me? Her anger condemns me to this life; facing loss and ignorance alone. Is a man still a father when his only child is gone?

What use is this? The same tormenting words whirl around in my brain again and again.

I walk my usual route, down the sloping hill of my garden out to the dirt track that eventually becomes a path. I am hemmed in on one side by a forest, the other by the mountains. The path leads to the main road and on to the mountain trail. Locals tell me this part of Munster is always rough and bare this time of year. I do not remember seeing it any other way.

As I walk, I see Maeve. She makes me smile with her cheerful wave. Her eyes that sing of better times.

"*Bonjour Monsieur,*" Her feeble efforts in my native language are forgiven in an instant. She laughs like a teenager on summer vacation, shaking the hair away from her face.

"*Dia dhuit,*" I reply. I have not grappled with the local language beyond this greeting. We stop to talk. A review of the year and hopes for the one to come; then on I walk. I want to ask her to walk with me. I have long wanted to ask her.

The slope of the mountain causes pain in the calves of my legs, but I relish it. The pain distracts me from the permanent cleft in my heart. I push myself, sorry now I did not take my walking stick. From the top of the hill I look back at the village, my home for the last seven years. I see Maeve make her way to the shop. She will

59

work there all day. Making customers smile, laugh, and spend a little more money than they planned. I turn to face the other way and look out to the sea. As I stand in the place where my little Cecile was last seen, I stare across the Atlantic. Sandrita is there somewhere, no doubt with her new lover. Foolish hope causes me to wonder; is Cecile with her?

To think she might be alive and happy with her mother is a two-sided weapon that gives pain and pleasure together as it stabs me again.

I sit from the exhaustion of grief, and I sleep.

I hear a voice calling my name. I cannot see anyone, and I am confused. Maeve appears.

She is breathless from her run up the mountain.

"Matt, Matt, there's ..." She catches her breath. "There's a letter. From America."

It is my turn to struggle to breathe.

"The postman tried your house but couldn't find you. He came straight to the shop to see if you were with me. You have to sign for it. Matt, you have to come now. MATTHIEU!"

Her raised voice forces air into my lungs and I grab her hand. It is only later I treasure the postman's instinct to look to Maeve to find me. For now, all other thoughts are suspended as we navigate the downward slope of the hill. The companionship, the fear and excitement are great as we run, step, and slide down to the flat road to the village. Hand in hand we take big strides, too afraid to run. Four people are waiting in the shop. There have never been six people in the shop at the same time. I sign for the letter and Maeve rushes her service to the customers. No time for tempting them to an extra purchase. Her goal now, to empty the shop.

I finger the letter, recognising Sandrita's writing. Our divorce long completed, no money issues to be resolved, there is only one reason she would write. I curse myself for the hateful thoughts I harboured against her. How could I believe she would be so cruel as to keep news of Cecile from me? I am, as she claimed many times, a hateful man. I gently stroke my own name and address. This letter may well be the joy of my life or the end of all my hope. This moment I have seen in the distance, like a black cloud on the horizon, never moving closer, crashes like a sudden thunderstorm.

I look at Maeve. She is breathless, smiling with hope and fear. I hold the letter out to her and she shakes her head.

"No, I can't."

"You must. Maeve; my hands will not obey me."

"No. It might be wonderful news; but what if it isn't? Don't ask me to be the person to tell you news that might break you."

"If you love me, you must."

Maeve's face reddens, and she avoids my eyes; the shop feels ever smaller.

"You know?"

"Of course I know; and it makes you the person who *must* be the one. Please."

Maeve takes the letter and as she does there is subsidence in my belly. She takes a small knife and slides it along the inside of the envelope. It takes a lifetime for her to get from one edge to the other. I watch her hands and my insides calm. I know there is no rush now. She takes the letter out and unfolds it. I can smell Sandrita; her hand cream, or do I imagine it? Maeve reads, slowly at first, then I watch her eyes hurry across the page, inhaling every word. She looks up at me and I hold my breath.

It all happens frame by frame. Maeve's face pales, like someone taken from the sea, like my Cecile. She takes a step forward and holds out her hand, but before she reaches me, she doubles up. A sound comes out of her like the cry of a wounded animal. I jump to stop her reaching the floor and she is in my arms. Sobbing. Apologising. Fighting with me for making her be the one. My heart breaks for Maeve, not myself. She clings to me, shaking and sobbing.

A customer comes into the shop and I send him back out with one gesture. I move to ease the deadening pain in the arm supporting

Maeve's weight, but it does not relieve the agony. The truth of the loss of my child starts to wash over me; that it brings such pain to the woman I love is bitter relief. Eventually she lifts herself up and we sit side by side.

She tells me Cecile's body was finally found three weeks ago. As we had suspected, she drowned in the sea, most probably after falling off the cliff side. The arguments between Sandrita and I, the mutual blame about who thought who was watching Cecile, they are well worn. She escaped both our notice and had gone higher up the mountain, to where we three used to walk together to pick wild heather.

Maeve closes the shop and we walk hand in hand back to the spot where I had been when she found me. We say a prayer together for my darling Cecile. Then we sit, holding each other. I am in less pain than I have been for some time. The bearer of my bad news is already the healer of my soul.

We can now bury Cecile. Sandrita's letter holds a promise to come and we will say goodbye properly.

Maeve and I will continue to heal each other. We will come to this place often to pick wild heather and think of Cecile; how she brought us together.

Wartime Roses
(Written for the 2014 Kilcullen
Great War Commemorative Group event
Our Unfortunate Sons)

I open my eyes to the whitest light, a glare. Am I in heaven? No. I remember my grandmother telling me all pain would end in heaven, and I'm in pain, great pain, a throbbing, and a dread comes upon me. I imagine the pain is away at a far-off place and I've yet to feel its worst. So, no. Not heaven.

My legs feel as though two hundred men are marching across the bones. Could it be I am still on the battlefield, and they think I am dead? I don't want to look but how can I not? I lift my head, but neither the marching men, nor my legs are there; just bandages that look like they have been stained by the dye of a thousand poppies. I cry out in despair and the white light shines over me again. It is not light itself; it is the uniform dress of the nurse. She is at my bedside with a smile that has no business in this pit of misery. It's a smile from another world, a place many miles from here.

She lifts my head to drink, her hand helping mine to hold the glass. She is a rose, blooming in a desolate place. Through the water I see her fingers, fine and pale, gently holding my rough hand. The water washes grit down my throat. At first it scrapes, but clean water follows it and for a moment I am refreshed. I look again to the empty space where pain lives; I feel weak. I am not dead, but I think I may be in hell. Can you be in hell and still be alive? The pain is different now. Not worse, nor is it better; it is just different. It is dull, yet I still fear its ability to overwhelm me.

It's days since first I saw the light, and the sight of it now brings a greater relief to me than any medicine it administers. Yesterday, her hair fell from one side of her cap as she was washing me. It brushed across my face for a second before she swept it back into place. She apologised a dozen times. Did she not understand a starving man would not expect to hear apologies for the provision of even a small but satisfying meal? Today though, she weeps as news of the death of her own sweetheart reaches her. She was to be married six weeks after the war started. What kind of man was he? Why did he not marry her before he left for France? I too receive a letter; from my mother. A blessing from God himself, but I see my nurse across the room as I read, and I know she brings as much comfort to me now as my mother ever could. Or is it maybe a different comfort?

That night we are all woken by a din from across the room. A fellow soldier is crying out, begging not to be sent back to the front. He is terrorised by a form invisible to the rest of us. My nurse is at his side, he thinks she is his younger sister. She does not argue, assuring him she and their mother are safe. She cradles her new brother's head as he calls the name 'Alice', again and again. In her role as sister, she agrees with him. When dread has stripped him of the strength to tremble, he sleeps.

A new day and a number of men leave, ready to be repatriated. Only half of me longs for home; only half of me will get there. The waves and tears as we left will have been put away now. I marched out of my village, but I will be carried back into it, to looks and stares and, God forbid, pity. Anything but pity.

The soldier from the bed beside me is now in a wheelchair. As he is wheeled away, he makes an attempt to salute with half an arm. I lock eyes with him and sit up as straight as I can to return the honour. We did not speak a word while we were neighbours; but what of it? He is my comrade. What words are needed when we share an experience that cannot be described, and carry memories impossible to discuss.

I awake the next morning to find my new neighbour has all his limbs. He is unusual in that. There is a bandage over his eyes and I hear him crying as the doctor explains to him he will probably never see again. The screen is moved away, and my nurse is there, reassuring him and encouraging him to rest. She turns to me and smiles her smile of light again. For a moment I am transported from this trench.

I can now sit up for most of the day. My neighbour has no injuries other than his blindness, so we talk. He tells me of his wife, and his son he has never seen, and never will. Their boy, Ralphy, was born ten weeks after Ralph Senior left for France. A letter with a photo of the infant with his mother arrived just after the poisoned gas took his sight. He asks me to describe his son. What do I know of babies? I say he is big and as I look closely, has his father's stick-out ears. My neighbour laughs and weeps. I tell him his wife is beautiful, and she holds their son with joy and pride. I tell him he should be a proud father and husband. I'm not sure whether it lessens or increases his melancholy; but from across the room I catch sight of my nurse. She is smiling and nodding, I think I am doing well.

It is my turn, and I speak of my dear mother and sisters. I tell him of my brother who wants to join the army but is too young to enlist. We both thank God for the blessing my brother does not welcome. I talk of my home on the farm and my now lost hope of taking over the running of the land after the war. He asks about a sweetheart and my eyes search for my nurse as I slowly shake my head. Though he cannot see it, he senses my hesitation. I admit I'm hopeful of finding love one day, but I do not own up that my hope is in this very ward.

Today, I get to feel the sun on my skin; I am not sure how long it is since I was outdoors. Yellows, reds, blues and pinks; green grass that shines like it has been polished. The air on my face is soft as silk and I fill my lungs with it. For months all I saw was brown and grey. Even the blankets on my bed shared the hue of the mud of the battlefield. This burst of colour revives me. When I return indoors my rose is just finishing changing the linen on my bed. I ask her to stay and talk a while, but she tells me her superior would not approve of her stopping for idle chat. I try to convince her it would not be idle and would add greatly to my recovery. The fresh air, the surge of hope it has given me, has emboldened me and I see her blush as she walks away, trying to hide her smile.

Another week has passed and news comes that I am ready to travel. I long for home and the touch of my mother's hand, but I feel my condition will worsen without the sight of my rose every day. I am determined to talk to her. I will ask her permission to write to her after I return home. An orderly has been teaching me how to manoeuvre the wheelchair myself. I ask him the name of my rose but he does not know which nurse I am talking about. I tell him she attended to the soldier with shell shock and she also was with my neighbour when he learned he was blind. He promises to investigate for me.

The day has come for me to leave and I am still none the wiser as to the name of my rose. The orderly comes back to me one last time to tell me that the events I gave him involved two different nurses. I insist he is wrong and tell him she has attended to me every day of my recovery. He says it is impossible to have had the same nurse all the time. They work on rosters and move around the field hospital. The doctor is now listening to our conversation and he agrees with the orderly. There would have been a number of different nurses tending to me over the weeks.

As I am wheeled out towards the transport vehicle I see them all. My roses. Those who are not busy smile and wave. I realise I have not fallen in love with one woman, but with all of them.

I will take their essence of loving care with me; a bouquet of memories. I will carry their fragrance home, and heal. I owe them that much.

Inspired by the chorus of a song I heard many times as a child, dedicated the wounded and fallen of World War I, and those who cared for them.

The Rose of No Man's Land
(Jack Caddigan/James A. Brennan)

There's a rose that grows on no-man's land
And it's wonderful to see;
Though it's spray'd with tears, it will live for years
In my garden of memories.
It's the one red rose the soldier knows
It's the work of the Master's hand,
Mid the war's great curse, stands a Red Cross nurse,
She's the rose of no-man's land.

Nanny and Albert

Lady Alexandra Morcombe enjoyed skipping across the landing. Nobody was there to tell her to stop, and how unladylike it was. The sight of the partially open nursery door transformed her skipping to an acceptable sedate walk. She stopped to look in. There was Nanny, singing to her baby brother Albert as he bobbed about over the woman's shoulder. She stared at the new Nanny's back. Alexandra knew *that* baby was here only because SHE was here. They arrived the same day, so she must have brought him; neither of them was welcome. Alexandra's mother and father saw the baby for an hour a day when he was fed, clean and happy. The rest of the time he was a loud smelly thing. But worse than that, since he had arrived, Lord Morcombe had stopped commenting on the beauty of her curls and how tall she was getting. He would walk around the drawing room carrying Master Albert, "My son, my boy," he'd say, as he introduced the new-born to his library and his precious antique bureau. Two things Alexandra was strictly prohibited from approaching.

The day father stepped on Constance was the last straw for Alexandra. Her father swore, and kicked the doll across the room, stating that dolls were not permitted out of the nursery. Her mother ran to Master Albert to make sure he had not been inconvenienced in any way. Alexandra picked Constance up, smoothed her hair, and rocked her to give them both comfort.

Alexandra's eyes tightened as she hovered near the nursery door, remembering that awful day. She scowled at Albert whose eyes were heavy as Nanny sang to him. She saw Nanny move and shudder at a slight cool in the room. Alexandra was silently out of sight before Nanny turned to close the nursery door.

In the school room, Madame Picout was pacing the floor when her pupil arrived, scolding her, *en Français,* for her tardiness. Alexandra pouted and sighed as she sat. The governess took her chair by the window and they began. Alexandra had perfected reciting her French verbs in a monotonous but lilting tone, and like clockwork, Madame Picout was asleep by '*allez*' in the future tense. The steady gentle snores confirmed it was safe and so, without taking her eyes off the teacher, Alexandra reached underneath her chair and produced Constance. Together they would come up with a plan to rid the house of Nanny and Albert.

A week later, Alexandra was sitting on the floor by the top of the servants' staircase. Pressing her face against the wall, she was just about able to see the top of their heads. Three of the servant girls stood in a huddle whispering and giggling. The arrival of Mrs Dolby, the housekeeper, from her sitting room sent them scuttling away; though thankfully not up the stairs. Nanny followed Mrs Dolby to the bottom of the stairs. She was carrying a suitcase in each hand. She put the suitcases down, took out a handkerchief and wiped her eyes.

"I just do not know how it happened Mrs Dolby," Nanny wept as she tied her bonnet under her chin.

"Don't you worry Nanny. You will get a good reference, I think it helped that you gave notice yourself, as soon as it happened. I am sure they will be discreet, and you will soon get another position."

"I do not think I will ever care for another infant again, Mrs Dolby." Nanny waved her handkerchief. "I do not know where all the pins have gone. I thought I had secured it. But the sight of Master Albert's soiled napkin falling off, and all of the mess falling all over Lord Morcombe's ..." Nanny could not finish her sentence for the tears. Mrs Dolby helped her on with her coat and walked her to the servants' door.

Alexandra made her way back to the drawing room.

"Here she is," said Lord Morcombe as she entered. "Where have you been? We missed you. Look at you, you are getting so tall."

Alexandra beamed at her father. She walked to the space where her father's bureau used to be and paced around the area of carpet marked out by its missing shape.

"Look at Alexandra's curls, my dear," said her father, walking around the room, ignoring the bassinet as he passed it.

Alexandra followed her father, stopping to look in the bassinet at her baby brother.

"A very plain name I thought," mused Lady Morcombe.

"Pardon my dear?" replied her husband.

"Nanny. Did you know her name was June Smith?"

Lord Morcombe grunted and looked towards where his bureau used to be.

Alexandra snatched a glance at her parents, both were lost in their contemplations. She reached into the bassinet, and whispered, "She is gone. And you will be next," as she tucked a handful of napkin pins under the end of his blanket.

Them That's Got Shall Get
(First Published NFFD Flashflood 2016)

Frankie turned the truck off the main road onto a dirt track. Passing crop fields, she sped towards the barren land ahead of her. Different now, but still familiar. Half a mile away, a combine harvester was chewing its way across a field. There was nothing else to see but the cloud of dry dirt following the truck.

The house eventually came into sight. Its apparent closeness always fooled newcomers, but Frankie knew the journey would take her another ten minutes.

Meg had seen the truck. She didn't recognise it but figured it must be Frankie. She was back out on the porch with two glasses of lemonade by the time Frankie got to the yard.

"That's a good sign," said Frankie. "Harvester in the north field. Who've you got working it?"

"It's Rayburn's field now. Sold it to him six months ago."

"Well, he's wanted it long enough."

"Yeah, Rayburn always gets what he wants eventually." Meg spat the poison from her tongue.

Frankie was tempted by the porch chair and the lemonade, but stayed standing.

"This is the last time Meg."

Meg refused to make eye contact and continued to move gently on the porch swing.

"I mean it. I won't keep doing this." Frankie took the new-born from the makeshift crib, and Meg stilled the swing.

Frankie's truck started with a roar. Meg watched the cloud of dust travel back down the dirt road. When it disappeared, she let the swing move again.

Billy Tongs

"Your nan's hair is exactly the same as my nan's hair."

"Wot?"

"Your nan's hair, it's exactly the same as my nan's hair. And Benzo's nan. All the nans come out of that hairdressers looking the 'zact same."

Tommy Miller stopped picking at the chewing gum stuck to the sole of his shoe and looked at his friend.

"Wot are you on about?"

"Nothing, come on." Billy jumped down from the wall.

"Hang on, I've nearly got this." Tommy held his tongue between his teeth as he peeled the last of the chewing gum off his shoe, sticking it to the wall as he jumped down.

"Where to now, Billy Boy? Up town to see what girls are about? Or we could go to the football field. Bradders has hockey training there today. We could slag him off from the side line."

"Let's walk home the long way, through town." Billy was already walking that direction.

"I knew you'd say that. Why do you always want to walk home through town? I'm not going all that way. It's another hour's walk and it's sausage, egg and chips for tea tonight. I'll see you tomorrow." Tommy dragged his heels for a couple of steps then started to kick an invisible football down the road.

"Yeah, see ya Tommy mate."

Billy was glad to be rid of Tommy. He always preferred to walk through town on his own. Tommy never stopped talking, and Billy couldn't concentrate with Tommy about.

He kept a good pace as he made his way, but slowed down when he reached civilisation. As soon as he began to pass people, it started. He did not see fat and slim, big ears and beards, limps and strides. He could only see hairstyles.

Short back and sides, grey rinse and set dry, asymmetrical bobs, crew cuts, flat tops, long layers, step cuts, grown out perms and faded colours. He would guess how 'old' someone's haircut was; how soon before their roots would need doing and what blade number had been used on short cuts. He would imagine at what angle the hair would need to be held to cut the layers in it and what size rollers were used to get a certain type of curl.

He had managed to keep it secret. He didn't know why, but he knew it was weird. He daren't tell Tommy. When Tommy found out Bradders had joined the hockey team, he gave it to him non-stop for six months. That was two years ago and he still wasn't done with him.

He was afraid to tell his mam, because he knew she'd be delighted. She had always wanted to be a hairdresser but never got there. She was a cleaner in the shopping centre. That meant discount hair dos in the salon and taking old hairdressing magazines home. Billy's mam never read women's magazines. There was no *Take a Break*, or *Woman's Way*; it was all *Hair Today* and *Style Secrets* in Billy's house.

He got to the shopping centre and took his place on the bench opposite the salon. After about 20 minutes, his mam came along with her trolley of cleaning products and mops.

"Billy! I love when you come to see me in work. It makes my day, it really does." She bear hugged him and as she did he turned her slightly so as not to miss the blow-dried with straighteners blonde highlights leaving the salon.

"I'm finished early today; now actually," she said with excited relief. "And guess what?! I get my raise today. So, I'm going to buy something I shouldn't for our tea. How does that sound Billy?"

"Brilliant mam, thanks."

"Before that, I'm going to treat myself to a half price blow dry. Come with me, will you? You can tell me all about your day, then we'll stop at the chippy on the way home."

"No mam, I'll get chips and go home. I'll put them in the oven. And the plates will be nice and warm when you get home." The last place Billy wanted to be was in the hair salon. Not with his mam.

"Oh, come on love. I could be an hour. It looks busy in there. Come and chat to me while I wait. I never get an early finish like this."

Billy could never say no to his mam when she begged him with a pleading voice and beautiful smile. She was right, it looked busy. Maybe he wouldn't be noticed.

When they got into the salon, it was chaos and Billy loved it. The place was packed – Tuesday special of *half price everything* was always popular. Billy and his mam sat down on the plush velveteen sofa after a hasty nod from a flying receptionist that said she knew they were there. There were women sitting at each basin, plus one or two that were seated in a holding area. The receptionist was running back and forward from basin to reception every time the phone rang.

Billy hid himself behind the latest edition of *London Hair* looking at the latest cuts, figuring out how they worked. Fifteen minutes later his mam was still waiting for her hair to be washed. Billy tried to swap magazines quickly, but he was spotted.
Rochelle (real name, Rita) the receptionist spotted him.

"Billy? Billy, oh fantastic. Thanks so much for coming in. Cheryl-Anne, Billy's here. Will I put him on basins? You've saved the day, you little beauty."

Cheryl-Anne (real name, Brenda) left her half rollered customer and ran to the waiting area. She pulled Billy up off his chair for his second bear hug of the day. Billy looked at his mam who was frozen to the spot, her mouth bobbing open and shut.

"We won't keep you too long now Janice," said Cheryl-Anne. "Not sure why our Saturday junior is here on a Tuesday, but we're really glad he is."

77

"Billy, can you rinse those two perms off and then you can shampoo Janice for me." Cheryl-Anne was back putting rollers in before she had finished her sentence.

Billy went to the basins and rinsed the two perms. Every so often he looked at his mam who was smiling at him. By the time he was ready to shampoo his mam's hair, he was relaxed and not afraid anymore.

"Is the water okay for you Janice?" he asked.

The Elephant in the Room

Sofia's camomile tea spilled out on the marble counter. "Muriel, you do know there's an elephant at the bottom of the garden, don't you? Traipsing around your petunias."

"What? What on earth are you talking about?" Muriel almost dropped the tureen of seafood chowder. Kicking off her mules, she was in her garden shoes and running down the lawn before Sofia could stop her, shooing and whooshing the elephant out of the flowerbed.

The elephant took two slow steps and a relieved Muriel made her way back to the house.

"Should I call pest control?" Sofia asked.

"Why dear?" Muriel slipped back into the mules.

"Because of the Indian elephant in your garden."

"He's an African elephant, Sofia darling."

"Oh, I'm sorry I didn't realise."

"That's quite alright. More camomile?"

"Yes, I'd love some. That chowder smells lovely."

Missing

Cara's phone rang for the third time in ten minutes. Lisa was used to her leaving the room to answer it, but this was different. Lisa watched her through the window, searching for a facial expression that would give away what was happening. Cara's face was set; rare swift nods the only evidence there was someone on the other end of the phone.

Lisa was propelled off her chair when a flash of Cara's eyes met hers. Cara turned her back to finish the call. Lisa wanted to run out to her but couldn't lift her feet. When Cara returned, Lisa could see she was composing herself.

"What? Tell me."

"Lisa, please sit down for a minute."

"Just tell me."

"That was Inspector Andrews. They found a boy who matches Rory's description."

"Alive or dead?"

"Lisa, I have to take you straight to …"

"ALIVE OR DEAD?"

"They're working on him."

*****

A week after his twelfth birthday, Rory Fogarty left his home for Gaelic football training, but he had not arrived. Nor had he come home. Since then, Lisa Fogarty saw little other than vapour trails in front of her. Faces were distant, voices were slow and hard to understand. Even though she knew what people were saying to her, it was as if she had to translate it before she could answer. Teary-eyed neighbours had been coming non-stop, with food and helpless looks.

81

So had the questions: endless questions with only one answer. "I don't know."

It had been just Lisa and Rory since he was two, when Rory's dad, Jack, decided parenting wasn't for him. He left them for London and a chance to make his fortune as a musician, leaving nothing behind but a hastily written note. Lisa hadn't heard from him since. Jack was no loss. Lisa often said that from the day Rory was born, he was more mature than his father. Detectives questioned her for hours about Jack, but it was a dead end. The note he left was the last trace of his existence in her world.

There was a sense of urgency in the first two days. Cara was the appointed family liaison officer, helping Lisa to understand what was going on, and giving her as much information as she could about the investigation. Detectives searched the house, tearing Rory's room apart. Lisa's computer was taken away, and her car was examined by a forensic team. She hated them crawling all over her house, repeating their questions. By day four, there were no questions left. She had welcomed the quiet at first, but was weary of it now.

The information they found about Rory's online activity was a blow to Lisa. He was on Facebook, from which she had banned him. Her computer showed he had signed up from there but had been accessing it somewhere else for a few months. When his friends were finally convinced that telling the truth was not a betrayal, they confessed he'd been borrowing their laptops and smartphones. After his birthday, Rory hadn't needed to borrow their devices anymore. He told his friends someone had sent him a tablet computer as a gift.

Lisa threw up when she heard this news and had to be sedated. When she could talk again, she confirmed she had no idea where the tablet had come from, or even that he had one. Guilt, anger and fear jostled for space in her head; at times, it was paralysing.

*****

Sirens and flashing lights at her gate brought neighbours to their doors again. Some were weeping. Lisa was escorted down her drive, Cara on one arm, another female police officer on the other. As she walked through her gate she saw the flowers and tributes to Rory. Teddy bears, photos of him in school and with his team, candles, his team jersey, cards that read 'WE LOVE YOU RORY', 'Come home soon, Rory', 'You'll never walk alone, Rory'. She stumbled into Cara, who got her into the car before the photographers could get any closer.

Lisa looked out of the window as they passed shoppers and kids on their way home from school.

"Look at them," she said to no one. "Everyone is acting like the world is normal, no hurry or panic. Did I used to be like that?"

They drove past the Gaelic football field. A place she had stood in all weathers, shouting his name, cheering his success, encouraging him in failure. She closed her eyes; that life was gone now.

Photographers crowded the car as it pulled up outside A&E. Questions were flung at her as she got out. Cara pushed her through the crowd. Just before they got to the door, one question rose above all others, landing on Lisa with force.

"Ms Fogarty, Ms Fogarty, Jack Jones was arrested in Dublin City Centre this morning; have you any comment? Was Rory taken by his father?"

Lisa swung around to a lightning storm of camera flashes before Cara pushed her through the door. Once they were inside, Lisa shook herself from Cara's hold. The ground under her feet was no longer solid, and she stumbled. Cara reached out her hand; Lisa pushed it away. Before she could say anything, a doctor arrived and hurried Lisa to a private room.

Apart from the tubes and wires, Rory looked perfect. She ran to him. She kissed his head, telling him how sorry she was.

"He is severely dehydrated, Ms Fogarty. There are signs of some minor damage to his kidneys. All we can do now is wait."

"Nothing … else?" Lisa could barely ask. "Nothing else happened to him?"

"No Lisa, nothing at all. He just needs lots of fluid and rest."

Lisa thanked him with a tear-filled nod, and allowed herself to breathe.

Inspector Andrews arrived, and Lisa reluctantly left Rory's side to speak to him.

"We found him in the trailer of a lorry. He'd been there for five nights. Without the energy drink he had in his kit bag, he wouldn't have survived. A roadie found him this morning and rang an ambulance straight away."

"Jack?" Lisa could hardly say his name.

"We have him in custody. The lorry was carrying equipment for his band. They're in Dublin for some gigs. He asked for a lawyer straight away, but Lisa, he is insisting that Rory sought him out."

"No! No way. Rory has never had any interest in his father."

"Well, Jack said he has no idea how Rory found him, or how he ended up in the trailer. He did admit they've been chatting online for a while. Jack said Rory's a clever kid, and he likes him. Rory told him you didn't like him being online, so he sent him the tablet to make contact easier."

Lisa winced under the weight of another wave of guilt.

"He said he did tell Rory about the Dublin gigs but denies knowing that Rory was coming to see him."

"And you believe that?" It was all too big for Lisa, and she struggled to hold herself upright.

"If he's lying, we'll find out."

*****

"So, how is he today?" Inspector Andrews had asked Lisa to the police station to give her an update.

"He's a little stronger. He took some food yesterday, but he still won't talk. Four days and I can't even get him to make eye contact with me."

"Give him time, Lisa; he's been through a huge trauma. He'll come through it. You both will."

"Jack was never a good father, but how …? How could he do this to such a beautiful boy?" Lisa grasped her coffee cup to steady her hands and stared through the liquid.

"That is why I asked to see you. We've interviewed all the members of the band and the security team at the venue. They're all confirming Jack's story. There was no suspicious behaviour from him. He told them about Rory but never mentioned meeting him or taking him."

"What about the tablet? He was grooming him on the internet."

"Jack gave us access to all his online accounts. The correspondence was scrutinised. There's no sign of any inappropriate conversations, no mention of them meeting up. There is nothing we can charge him with."

"NO!" Lisa was up off her chair. "Rory would never have done this without encouragement. Jack must be culpable! My child was locked in a trailer for five days."

"We spoke to the roadie who opened the trailer and found Rory. He locked the trailer himself on the evening Rory went missing. CCTV confirms that no one went near it again until he opened it and found Rory. Jack wasn't involved, Lisa. We can't hold him any longer."

*****

The sound of Rory's voice woke her. It was weak, but he was back.

"Mam? Mammy. I'm sorry, Mammy."

Lisa climbed on to the bed beside him. "Hey there, you don't have to be sorry about anything."

85

"I just wanted to meet him. I just wanted to see him. I'm sorry, Mam."

"I know, love." She kissed his hair. "I know you did, and you don't have to be sorry for that either."

"Is he coming? Is my dad coming to see me?"

Lisa looked up at Cara and Andrews, who had just arrived. She asked them the same question with a look; Andrews just shook his head.

"No, sweetheart." She brushed a hair from Rory's face. "I don't think so."

Reception

By 8.47am she had already taken seven calls and not one of the company reps seemed to want to make any sales. So much for the recent memo about the 8.30 SHARP start. She could hear half of them in the kitchen, waiting for their turn with the kettle; conversations about how long the week was, the beer they were looking forward to on Friday and the surprise of a fish and chip supper the previous night, even though it was only Wednesday.

"I'm sorry sir, I still can't get an answer from that line. Can I take a message? Probably in an early team meeting, let me take your number and I'll get someone to call you back."

The callers could not have missed the loud laughter from the kitchen. She was embarrassed now, saying "Sorry that line is engaged," when the distinctive chortle of the person whose extension she was trying filled the ground floor of the building.

The phones went quiet at ten past nine, by which time all had drunk their coffee and were at their desks. She looked out of the window. Her view from the office was not pretty. Metal fences, portacabins, portaloos, badly parked cars. But over it all stood a structure she loved to look at, the Transporter Bridge.

Her memories of the bridge were many and mixed, but she did love to look at it. Her father had often taken her across as a foot passenger when she was a child. She'd had her first kiss with Hywel Davies on it. And her childhood friend Abbie had told her sad secrets as they climbed it on Sundays or Bank Holiday Mondays.

The phone brought her back and she tried four extensions before she was able to release the call to someone.

She remembered Abbie's tears as she told her about her parents separating and the horrible man her mother had brought in as a replacement dad. Abbie's dad was a funny, zany man. Abbie said it was like living with a comedian. He left Abbie's mother when he found someone who would laugh at his jokes. Her mother had obviously found someone else to laugh with. Abbie didn't laugh again for a long time.

A surprisingly large amount of post arrived for the office and that kept her busy for an hour, sorting it and date stamping it.

"What's that tune?" Dai Wrench shouted from the kitchen.

"Sorry?" she said.

"That tune you're humming? I can't remember the name."

She hadn't noticed her own humming.

"It's a Lloyd Webber isn't?" said Dai stirring his tea. "*Cats*, I think. The wife dragged me to see it. Not bad actually. Midnight not a doo bee dee moonlight, da da dee dee dee daa da..." he sang, walking off with his tea.

Abbie's Dad had an LP of Lloyd Webber tracks and it would always be on when they came back from their bridge walk. They'd sing along sharing Abbie's dried-up dinner, scraping the congealed gravy off the plate. She looked out of the window longing for the bridge carrier to move. It rarely did these days and never on a weekday.

A stream of phone calls brought her musing to an end and she dialled several lines, taking messages for most.

The next time she looked up she saw someone walking across the top of the bridge. She would hardly have noticed except they were in a bright yellow coat. Maybe a bridge worker in a high-vis jacket? Even from the distance she was sure it was a woman.

The walker stopped in the middle, looking over as if attempting to climb down. For a moment Katie's blood ran cold, thinking the woman was going to jump, but she just stood there. Then she began to tie something to the bridge. It unfurled in the wind and was blowing about, making it impossible to read. Katie had seen happy birthday banners on bridges and barriers, but never on this bridge. She was so angry that this person was going to deface this structure that was so precious to her. She fumed for a bit as the woman on the bridge worked on securing her banner. Katie found the number for Transporter Bridge maintenance and punched it in to her phone. Maybe one of their engineers might intervene to stop this. She waited anxiously as the phone rang, but as the line was answered she let the phone slip out of her hand. As the last corner of the sign was secured to their bridge, Katie could read ... 'Katie I miss you. My old friend, my best friend. Please call me on 0790910293. Love from Abbie.'

Katie ignored the ringing landline, laughing, crying and scrabbling in her handbag for her mobile.

Malcolm Fulcrum ENT Expert
(Shortlisted in the Jonathan Swift Creative Writing Award Oct 2018)

Malcolm Fulcrum was not where he'd planned to be. His dream was to be a surgeon, specialising in all things to do with ears, nose and throat. He'd had visions of being called Dr Fulcrum, then Mr Fulcrum; racing through long hospital corridors to the next nasal emergency, fending off the advances of pretty nurses; going home to Marjorie for his comforts. Instead he was an orderly in a small local hospital.

As a child, Malcolm had been obsessed with swallowing things, sticking things up his nose, and poking his ears. He'd spent a long time in the Paediatric ENT departments and thought there could be no finer profession than fishing a tiny plastic object from the facial orifice of a mischievous child.

Sadly, he did not get the grades needed to go to medical school. His first jobs were factory work, on temporary contracts. He was always relieved when they were over. He did a two-day stint on a building site which left him traumatised after seeing the dirty hands of builders stir tea with dusty spoons.

His employment support officer encouraged Malcolm to apply for the hospital porter job. He sold it well; encouraging Malcolm that though he would not be the man to do the work, he would be the one who delivered patients *to* the one who did the work. "A surgeon can't operate until the patient is delivered," the career guide would say. "You'd be the back-up guy. Still part of the team that makes things happen."

Malcolm could see it all. The surgical team scrubbed in, gowned and gloved, waiting in anticipation for him to charge in with the ready patient, making it all possible. He thought it could even be a back-door into medical school, or a shot at being a nurse. He really believed he could move up the chain. In reality however, Malcolm spent his time taking patients to the x-ray department, sneaking them out back doors for a smoke, and getting their newspapers for them from the kiosk. When he did bring patients to the surgical wing, they were taken off him without a word, or even eye contact. He had been doing it for twenty years. Marjorie didn't know how many times he'd re-applied for medical school. Eventually, one of the consultants who worked in the teaching hospital took him aside and advised him not to apply again, as it was getting embarrassing.

That was a bad day for Malcolm and in the ensuing discouragement and preoccupation, he got off the lift on the wrong floor and delivered a patient who was having a wart removed, to the Gastroenterology department for an enema. For weeks his colleagues would laugh as they told him not to worry, that it all came out right in the end.

Thankfully he kept his job, but he felt downgraded after that and was more recently working with very elderly people who were going from hospital to care homes. He knew others regarded it as grunt work, but he held on to that picture of being an important part of the process. He believed he could still give it his all. Until now.

Malcolm came home from his late finish. As usual, he checked the post, which Marjorie always left to him, while she got on with setting his supper out. There was only the one letter and he knew what it was. The one he was expecting, and dreading. He shoved it back into the envelope and threw it on the coffee table just in time for Marjorie to pop the lap tray down. He picked up a toasted marmite soldier, looked at it and sighed.

Marjorie went back to sewing buttons on to her latest knitted creation.

"I'm very concerned about the hostess trolley," she said, sorting through her button box. "It's not keeping the food hot. I was so embarrassed the night Barbara and Felix were here. The peas were definitely cold. Oh look, there's the last button I need for your new winter cardigan." She looked at her husband who had turned into a statue.

"Malcolm," she said, concerned. "Malcy?"

Marjorie called him again but there was no answer. She got off her chair and walked to him, still holding her sewing project. She put her hand on his shoulder and he jumped, sending the marmite soldier across the room onto the coffee table.

"Malcy, whatever is the matter with you?"

"I'm sorry, I'm so so sorry Dumpling," he said with a cry in his voice. "What a waste! What a terrible waste."

"Don't worry about that, I can make you more soldiers."

"No, not it's not that, Diddums. Although I do hate wasting food." He looked at the soldier, which had landed on the coffee table and was lying next to the letter. A rush of blood went to his head. He jumped up and shouted. "You know what else I hate? Wasting time! I've wasted my life Schmoopsie. I've wasted my life. You know what I wanted to be, and it will never happen. And today ... well I've just had the letter confirming it. I'm going to be made redundant."

Marjorie gasped at his outburst and fell to her seat on the sofa.

"I know, I'm shocked too, Pigeon," said Malcolm, pacing the floor, waving his arms and pointing. "A generous retirement package is what they are calling it, but what it means is I am being put out to pasture. Removed from all service, all evidence of my presence will be gone. It's good money I can't deny it, but what will I have left behind? I'll be a vague memory to one or two, but to most – nothing. Thirty days they've given me to respond. Well they can wait. I'm going to fight this. Fight it all the way."

Marjorie was nodding and shaking her head; banging the arm of the sofa, making silent defiant protests.

"You're right Precious. It's too soon, I'm not ready. What have I achieved? What have I done? Sweet Florence Aldershot, that's what. Excuse my French, Peachie. But really, I've taken the test of life, and I've failed. Well I'm going to achieve something before they retire

93

me out. I am not leaving that job until I know I've made a difference; to someone, anyone!"

Marjorie shook her head and waved her arms.

"I know Pushkin, I know. You remind me every day of the difference I make to the old dears I cart around, but it's not enough for me." Malcolm strode up and down the room. "There has to be more. Don't you understand that, Munchkin?"

Malcolm swung around to look at Marjorie who was now thumping her chest, her lips turning blue.

"Snookums!" Malcolm cried as he ran to her. She went limp in his arms. In a second, he stood her up, swished her around and talked himself through the steps as he did them …

"One foot in front of the other for balance, lean forward, make a fist with one hand, grasp the fist with the other hand, place under ribcage and pull inwards and upwards as you … THRUST …"

Once, twice, three times he did it with no success. Then on the fourth try, a large wooden button went flying across the room, landing on the coffee table, next to the envelope and the marmite soldier. Marjorie coughed for a while then eventually caught her breath. Malcolm ran to get her some water, then sat beside her holding her hand.

She gazed at him. He loved it when she looked at him like that.

"My Hercules," she said, with a scratch in her voice. "You saved me Malcy."

He looked back at her with the same adoration. "I did, didn't I Cabbage?" he said, kissing her hand.

They sat together for a while until Marjorie felt a bit better.

"I'd better tidy up," she said, eyeing the coffee table. "Look at the terrible mess we've made. What shall I do with this letter?"

Malcolm looked at Marjorie again, and was at once filled with a contentment that had eluded him for years. "Give it here, Sausage," he said. "I'm going to reply tomorrow and after I do, we're going shopping."

"For a new hostess trolley?" Marjorie clapped her hands together with elation.

"Absolutely, my Pumpkin Pie."

"Malcy," she cried, throwing her arms around him. "You really are my hero."

Thank you for reading my stories! Now that you've finished, please spare a few minutes to review *A Sense of the Sea and other stories* for Amazon and Goodreads. As an indie author, your feedback is invaluable to me.

Other publications by Annmarie Miles

The Long & The Short of it: Stories you will always have time for
Published November 2013, republished March 2018

Praise for The Long & The Short of it

Amazon Reviews

Miles has a beautifully light, conversational tone that reminds me a lot of Maeve Binchy, particularly Binchy's own short fiction. 4/5*

Thoroughly enjoyable and engaging read. If you like short stories you will love this book. 5/5*

Lots of humour and real Irish story telling. 5/5*

Poignant, funny and thought-provoking. I look forward to reading more from this author in the future. 5/5*

Contributions to other Publications

How I Learn edited by Helen Bullock

New Life: Reflections for Lent published by ACW

Merry Christmas: A festive feast of stories, poems and reflections published by ACW

Printed by Amazon Italia Logistica S.r.l.
Torrazza Piemonte (TO), Italy

13004244R00066